West made his way, slowly, toward the woman.

The coroner dropped a black bag on the ground opposite the deceased.

"Ma'am?" West tugged the material of his pants and crouched beside her. "I'm Sheriff West Garrett. I'm afraid I need to ask you a few questions."

The woman stilled. Her sobs ceased.

West rested his forearms on his thighs, allowing his hands to dangle between his knees. Rain dripped from the brim of his sheriff's hat and the sleeves of his slicker. "Are you hurt, ma'am?"

She raised her tear-stained face, slowly, catching his gaze in hers. "No."

"Tina." His heart clenched and gut fisted at the sight of her.

"Hi, West," she croaked. Her rain-soaked hair hung in clumps over her shaking shoulders.

The sound of his name on her tongue was a painful slap of nostalgia. "Hi." West struggled to make her presence at the crime scene something other than ludicrous. "What are you doing here?"

THE SHERIFF'S SECRET

JULIE ANNE LINDSEY

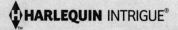

Dedicated to Tina.

ISBN-13: 978-1-335-52639-7

The Sheriff's Secret

Copyright © 2018 by Julie Anne Lindsey

Recycling programs
for this product may
not exist in your area.

Printed in U.S.A.

Julie Anne Lindsey is a multi-genre author who writes the stories that keep her up at night. She's a self-proclaimed nerd with a penchant for words and proclivity for fun. Julie lives in rural Ohio with her husband and three small children. Today, she hopes to make someone smile. One day she plans to change the world. Julie is a member of the International Thriller Writers (ITW) and Sisters in Crime (SinC). Learn more about Julie Anne Lindsey at julieannelindsey.com.

Harlequin Intrigue

Protectors of Cade County

Federal Agent Under Fire
The Sheriff's Secret

Visit the Author Profile page at Harlequin.com.

CAST OF CHARACTERS

Tina Ellet—When a gunman opens fire on the members of her group counseling session, this clinical psychologist is horrified to learn the shooter is also a stalker who has been watching her for months, and now he has her baby.

West Garrett—Cade County sheriff and first love of Tina Ellet, West is willing to do whatever it takes to protect her and bring her baby home safe, but staying focused on the job won't be easy with the secret he has burning in his heart.

Carl Morgan—A stalker in love with Tina Ellet, Carl will do anything to be part of her family, including lie, cheat and kill. Now he's got her baby, and it won't be long before he has Tina, too.

Lily Ellet—Tina's infant daughter, abducted by her mother's stalker and in need of a hero.

Cole Garrett—Youngest of four Garrett brothers, and a Cade County deputy, Cole is all in to back his brother and capture the stalker who has stolen Tina's baby.

Blake Garrett—FBI agent and oldest Garrett brother. Blake's no-nonsense approach to hunting criminals puts him shoulder to shoulder with his younger brothers, determined to get justice for Tina and bring her baby home safely.

Chapter One

Tina Ellet checked her watch for the tenth time in half as many minutes. Two of her seven patients had missed the entire group session, without so much as a text to let her know they weren't coming. Dedication and accountability to personal recovery was a must in her program, and the group had always taken the requirements seriously. Until now. So what were those two up to?

She rubbed goose bumps off her arms. Trouble was coming, she was sure of it. She just wasn't sure what form it would take. She approached her wide office windows and gave the empty sidewalk outside another long look. The forest of brightly colored trees across the lot swayed with a wicked wind. It wasn't autumn in Kentucky until a storm tried to knock you down. "Please take it slow on your way home or to work." She turned to face the group with a forced smile. "It doesn't look good out there."

The men and women nodded in easy agreement.

"If any of you hear from Carl or Tucker, please let them know they were missed." Tina was certain many of them were worried, too, but there was nothing to be done about it for now. Instead, they flattened folding chairs and dropped disposable cups into the trash, making fast work of the cleanup and sending faint scents of cigarette smoke and coffee into the air. The scents of her childhood, minus the distinct sting of alcohol.

When the room was righted, she shouldered her handbag and collected the empty tray from her homemade blueberry muffins. Early morning sessions were popular with her group, and Tina tried to send a little hope and encouragement with each member when they left. At least enough to help them face whatever the day might bring. So far, this day had brought plenty of rain. The forecasted showers had come right on schedule, successfully soaking everything in sight. "I suppose we might as well make a run for it. The rain doesn't appear to be giving up anytime soon." In fact, the rain hadn't slowed since it began more than an hour before. "Does everyone have a ride?"

Steven, the newest member of her group, looked away as the others raised their car keys.

"Steven?" She tipped her head toward the sheeting rain. "Would you like a ride home? I'm sure someone would be glad to drive you. No one should walk in this."

Several members chimed in with offers, and Steven dipped his chin in agreement to the one made by Carol, an older woman standing near the door. Carol winked at Tina. She'd see Steven home safely.

Sometimes heading a recovery group for PTSD and trauma survivors was tricky. What one member saw as comfort, another saw as a threat, and so far, Steven saw most things as a threat. He'd joined the group after receiving an other-than-honorable discharge from the army last month. His severe emotional trauma had led to unbecoming behavior that garnered him a quick boot from the service, complete with truncated benefits and nowhere to turn for the support he needed. Luckily, Tina had found him, and she was certain she could help, if she didn't scare him away first.

"All right. Here we go." She swung the door open and held it for the group to pass. Together, they moved onto the sidewalk and waited beneath the large metal awning while Tina locked up. Hopefully, wherever Carl and Tucker were, they were safe, not caught in a flash flood or car accident or worse. She blamed her "mother's mind" for the number of scary scenarios scooting through her head. Since the birth of her precious daughter four months ago, she'd begun to see potential danger everywhere and longed more than ever to wrap her arms around the entire world in protection.

Slowly, a few brave souls ventured into the storm, plodding through puddles toward their vehicles and prompting the others to follow. The lot was nearly empty this time of day, making Mountain Medical Plaza the perfect location for her private morning sessions.

Tina followed Carol and Steven toward a massive

pickup truck whose lights flashed and locks popped up upon approach. Tina's car was the small sedan two spots away. Steven slowed his pace as he neared Carol's truck, suddenly unconcerned by the rain and wholly focused on a distant point in the morning sky.

"Steven?" Tina lifted her handbag overhead, a makeshift umbrella, and squinted through the rain. "Everything okay?"

He raised an arm, finger pointed at the building's rooftop. "Do you see that?"

The fine hairs on the back of Tina's neck raised to attention. She forced her eyes to focus through the downpour. "What do you see?"

A small shadow rocked into view. What appeared to be the long barrel of a rifle stretched out before it.

Ice coiled in Tina's gut. *It couldn't be...*

"Gun!" Steven yelled. "Get down!" He turned for Tina, arms thrown wide as one loud blast of gunfire cracked the air. Steven's head whipped back and his gait fell short. His legs crumbled beneath him and his body collapsed onto the rain-battered asphalt in a silent thud. Group members screamed and hollered around her, scattering between vehicles and running for the building. Shattered glass rained over Steven, falling from the truck window at his side.

Tina's lungs burned as she struggled to breathe. She fell to the ground, barely perceiving what had happened. Wind whipped through her hair and mingled with the ringing in her ears. Voices warbled around her, distorted by the storm and panic beating through her head. "Stay down!" she screamed. "Get down and stay down!" She forced her eyes to search for the shadow once more, but it was gone.

Where did it go? She craned her neck in every direction, as if the shooter could be anywhere, beside her, behind her. Her chest ached and her mouth dried. How could she know who the next bullet would hit? Would there be another? Was the man finished shooting, or was he reloading? She dug her phone from her purse and dialed 911.

"911. What's your emergency?" a tinny voice echoed in her ringing ear.

Tina scrambled under the truck, counting pairs of feet moving through the lot toward the building. Four. Good. The rest were safe and together now.

"Ma'am? What's your emergency?" the voice repeated.

The world snapped back into focus then, the tragedy becoming unbearably clear. "There's a gunman at Mountain Medical Plaza." The words fell clumsily off her tongue, a line memorized for a play. Impossible to be real. "One man is down. I don't know." She stared at Steven's motionless form. "He's not moving. I don't know where he was hit. There's so much blood."

"Where's the shooter now?"

"I'm not sure. He stopped, I think." Tina willed her mind into focus. Her group needed her. Steven needed her.

"Are you somewhere safe now, ma'am? Is there somewhere you can find shelter until emergency responders arrive?"

Her office door seemed miles away, but two group

members were already there, crouched against the wall, and two others were steps away. She could help them. Get them inside.

Screaming tires drew her attention across the lot. A faded red pickup truck roared recklessly in the distance and fishtailed onto the county road beyond, barreling away like the devil was chasing it.

Tina pulled in a long gulp of oxygen to clear her brain. "I think the shooter is gone now. There was only one shot. Maybe two minutes ago. And someone's racing away in a pickup." She forced herself from beneath the truck and onto her knees, crawling over the broken glass to Steven's side. "A man's been shot. He's not moving." She stared at his motionless chest. "Not breathing." Tina pressed shaky fingers to his neck in search of a pulse that didn't beat, then tried again. "No, no, no, no." She set the phone on the ground at Steven's side, pressed the speaker option, then laced her fingers against his chest and said a silent prayer. Tina filled his lungs and pumped his heart for him until her arms shook uncontrollably from terror, grief and effort. "He's not breathing," she cried. "His heart isn't beating. CPR isn't working."

Behind her, the group bellowed for her to come to them. Above her, the thunder rolled.

Tina grabbed her phone and pushed onto her feet. In a torrent of desperation, she forced herself away from Steven. A round of ugly sobs pressed through her tightened lips as she hurried back to the group collecting outside her office once more. She wiped her hands on her shirt, smearing it with blood, then jammed her key into the lock and ushered the others inside. "One man is dead," she reported to the woman on the phone. "The rest of us are…" Are what? *Fine?* None of them were fine. A man had just been murdered in front of their eyes. "No one else was physically injured."

She wiped her eyes and nose, fighting the wave of panic determined to lay her in a useless ball. How many times had she called 911 as a kid? How many times had her drunken father taken his frustrations out on a mother too depressed to get out of bed? Broken limbs and noses. Cuts and bruises. Nothing like this. Never like this, and yet she'd felt exactly this way. Desperate. Afraid. And guilty. Always guilty. "I'm so sorry," she wept. "So very sorry."

The soft cry of an approaching ambulance registered in the distance, refueling her hope and drive. "I hear them now," she told the dispatch operator. "Help is almost here." She made the second announcement more loudly, aiming her words at the terrified group before her.

Tina slid her suit jacket from her shoulders. "You will survive this," she told them, falling back on her training. "Understand?" They stared in variations of shock, anguish and despair. "You are survivors." She forced the words from between clenched teeth, as much for her own benefit as theirs. "Help is almost here now. You're going to be okay."

Except Steven. Steven would never again be okay.

When she could find no more words, she carried her jacket through the raging storm and placed it over

Steven. Fresh out of faux strength, Tina fell onto her bottom beside him, cell phone in hand, and bawled. What was wrong with this world?

CADE COUNTY SHERIFF West Garrett pressed a wide-brimmed hat over his head and levered himself out of the cruiser. A carousel of red-and-white lights illuminated the gruesome scene at a local counseling practice. Blood and glass covered the lot beside a newer model pickup truck. EMTs spoke with a cluster of people near one building.

A man lay motionless and partially covered by a tiny, bloodstained woman's coat. This must have been the fatality Dispatch had announced. Presumably, the coat belonged to the woman curled up at the man's side. Her arms were wrapped around her knees and her face was buried in the material of her ruined suit pants. Only the top of her blond head was visible, and it was shaking with each new sob she released.

West made his way, slowly, toward the woman.

The coroner dropped a black bag on the ground opposite the deceased.

"Ma'am?" West tugged the material of his pants and crouched beside her. "I'm Sheriff West Garrett. I'm afraid I need to ask you a few questions."

The woman stilled. Her sobs ceased.

West rested his forearms on his thighs, allowing his hands to dangle between his knees. Rain dripped from the brim of his sheriff's hat and the sleeves of his slicker. "Are you hurt, ma'am?"

She slowly raised her tearstained face, catching his gaze in hers. "No."

"Tina." His heart clenched and his gut fisted at the sight of her after all these years, her clothes smeared in blood.

"Hi, West," she croaked. Her rain-soaked hair hung in clumps over her shaking shoulders.

The sound of his name on her tongue was a painful slap of nostalgia. "Hi." West struggled to make her presence at the crime scene something other than ludicrous. "What are you doing here?"

"It's my practice."

West rubbed a rough hand over his mouth. He'd heard she worked at the medical center but had refused the details. This wasn't the same girl who'd stolen his teenage heart and eventually destroyed it. That girl had left Cade County long ago. This was someone else. Someone he no longer knew. He pulled in a long breath and refocused on the job. He gave her a more critical exam. "Is any of this blood yours?"

"No." Tina pushed onto her feet with a whimper and wrapped trembling arms around her middle. "I'm not hurt. I want to help."

He stood, as well. "All right. You can start by telling me what happened." He motioned to a section of the sidewalk covered with an awning. "Let's step out of the storm."

She complied, shuffling toward the building, peeling clumps of sopping hair off her cheeks and forehead. "We were leaving the building. It was just after eight, and there was a shadow on the roof." She stopped short and swallowed several times.

"We?"

"I have a weekly support group for PTSD and emotional trauma survivors." She rolled her shoulders forward and squelched a sob. "Steven saw the figure on the roof. He told us to get down. He tried to get to me." She pressed the heels of both hands against her eyes. "The gunman shot him before he reached me."

West nodded toward the man on the pavement. "That is Steven?"

She removed her hands from her face with a sigh. "Steven Masters. He was discharged from the army about a month ago. He has a wife and little girl." Her voice broke on the last word. "Oh, Lord. His poor family," she whispered. Tina spun away from West, walking aimlessly into the lot, obviously in shock despite her efforts to look otherwise.

"Hey." West jogged to her side and wrapped an arm around her shoulders. "Why don't you have a seat while we talk?" He led her to a bench beneath the awning and released her at once. The instinct to comfort her was unprofessional and wildly outdated. "Better?"

She didn't answer.

"Tina?" West knew firsthand that she wasn't a sharer, but this time he needed her to open up. "I know this is tough," he began.

Tina rolled glossy blue eyes up at him. "Someone shot Steven from that rooftop. I don't know who. I don't know why." She shook her head roughly. "It's just nonsense."

"West?" His baby brother and current deputy, Cole Garrett, strode to his side. Cole was four years younger than West and twice as smart, but he'd been bitten by the law enforcement bug like the rest of the Garrett men and refused to go out and change the world like West and their older brothers had suggested. "I'm going to head out and see if I can get a bead on this guy."

"What do you have so far?" West asked.

Cole gave Tina a wayward look. "Not much. Witnesses heard a car hightailing out of here. I'm going to head up the road and see if anyone saw a vehicle taking the state route in a hurry."

"It was a pickup truck," Tina said.

Cole's sharp gaze locked on hers before drifting back to West. "Isn't she—"

"Don't," West warned.

Cole whistled the sound of a falling missile and walked away.

Tina rolled her head against the wall behind their bench. "I suppose I'm not exactly the Garrett family's favorite local."

West grunted. That was a conversation he never wanted to have. The past was the past. He'd like to leave it there. "I need to know which member of your group could've made someone mad enough to do this?"

Tina's soft expression hardened. She glanced at

the coroner's van. "The only person to blame is the maniac who did it."

West raised an eyebrow. "I'm not blaming. I'm looking for bread crumbs. Which one's the loose cannon?"

"All my patients are serious about their recovery. They're employed. Paying bills. Contributing to society. They wouldn't be here every week, carving out time before work, if they weren't dedicated to the process."

"Uh-huh." West nodded. "I understand why you'd say they're doing well, seeing as how you're their therapist." He gave a little smile, knowing he walked a fine line. "You look for the best in people, and that's admirable, but can you tell me honestly that if one of your patients had gotten into trouble, you'd know? How can you be sure? Because I'm sitting outside an office where people suffering from emotional distress come for treatment, and one of them is dead. You want me to believe the location is a coincidence?"

She scowled. "Of course it can't be a coincidence because you don't believe in those."

West regrouped and tried again before she shut him out completely. "You're right. You know these guys. I don't. I'll admit that, but I'm thinking distraught individuals tend to make poor decisions, and maybe one of them got tangled up with someone capable of doing this."

"No."

"No?"

She shook her head. "You're wrong about my group."

"How do you know?" West asked. "What do you talk about in your sessions? Has anyone shared anything out of the ordinary lately? Did they meet someone new? Make a friend? Take a trip?"

Tina rubbed her forehead. "That's all covered under counselor-patient confidentiality."

"Are you kidding me?" West bristled.

"You know I can't tell you any of those things."

West ground his teeth. "Even in the aftermath of all this, you still want to keep secrets?"

Tina looked away. "You can ask them anything you want to know. I'm sure they'll tell you. And I'll tell you anything I can about my day. About the moments before and after the shooting. About the figure. Anything that won't break my patients' trust, but I owe them that. I took an oath."

West braced himself for a long day. Prying secrets from Tina was a task he'd never had any success with, and frankly she was right. What he wanted to know was covered under confidentiality laws, unless she'd suspected criminal activity. In that case, she had an obligation to report it, but she'd already declared the group's united innocence and probably wouldn't change her story. "Okay," he conceded. "Fair enough. I'll ask my men to question the group members. What do you say about coming with me to the station while they do that? It sounds like you spoke to the victim just before the incident, and it seems you were also the closest to him by proximity." His gaze slid over the bloodstains on her rain-soaked blouse and pants. "I need to get an official report from you, and I'd like to continue the interview while the details are fresh. I imagine you'd like to get away from here for that."

"Yeah."

"Well, then, Miss Ellet, let me walk you to my car."

Chapter Two

Tina climbed inside the sheriff's cruiser, shaking off memories of similar rides as a girl. Every time her dad had caused a scene at a park or ball game and was hauled in for a night in the drunk tank, Tina was escorted home by a nice deputy, often by the former sheriff. West's dad. Eventually, she'd smartened up and steered clear of her dad before he could insist they go anywhere together.

She buckled in and winced as the condition of her hands and clothes registered. "Oh." She rubbed her stained fingers against the ruined material of her pants, but it was no use. A tremor rocked through her as memories of the gunshot came rushing back. Tina shook her hands out hard at the wrists and released a shuddered breath. "Can…" She swallowed against the painful lump in her throat. "Can we make a pit stop at my house? I'd like to get a dry change of clothes before we go to the station. I don't think I can concentrate like this." She bent and stretched her fingers in the air above her lap. "Please."

West gave the gas pedal a break, seemingly torn between giving her what she wanted and following his protocols. West had always been a stickler for doing the right thing, and that probably didn't allow for a trip to an old girlfriend's home before taking her formal statement.

"Which way to your place?" He dropped his sopping wet hat between them, then ran a hand through his hair.

She raised her brows in surprise. Maybe she wasn't the only one who'd been changed by time. "Left on Canyon Drive. We're in the River Park neighborhood." She balled her shaking hands into fists and set them on her lap.

"Who's we?" West asked, sweeping his gaze to her naked ring finger.

"Just Lily and I," she said. "My daughter." A hot tear stung the corner of one eye. Lily had come too close to being an orphan today. She pushed her focus beyond the passenger window. "And Ducky."

"Ducky?"

She sighed. "The dog."

"No Mr. Ellet?" he asked. "Or maybe you have a new last name?"

Tina touched the bare skin where a wedding ring had briefly dared to dream. "We weren't married long enough for me to get it changed. I hadn't realized there was a hurry." She turned her stricken face to his, chin up, jaw tight. "I met him about two years ago, right after I moved back to town. We were married after a few months, and he died four weeks later. I never got to tell him about Lily." She silently cursed her chattering teeth for betraying her show of strength.

West gave her a long, silent look. "How old is Lily?"

"Four months." Tina had seen the expression West was giving her before, though never from him. *Pity.* "It's fine. We're okay. He was here and gone like a dream. Sometimes, I think if it wasn't for Lily, I'd wonder if he was real." The pain was real. The loss. But it was true: her short time with Thomas had felt more like a movie she'd seen long ago than an adventure she'd truly been part of.

"I'm sorry about your loss. Lily's, too. Is she home now?"

"No." She batted stinging eyes. "She's at Mary's. That's the sitter." Somehow West's condolences to her daughter meant more to her than anything else he could have said.

"What happened?" West asked. "I'm not trying to pry. I'm just getting caught up. It's been a long time."

"I don't mind." It was strange being on the other side of a confessional for a change. Her spilling her troubles and someone else nodding patiently as the story unfolded. "Hunting accident."

"You didn't know him long before you married." A hint of agitation edged his voice. "Then he just died?"

"Basically," she answered. "He went up to the mountains for the weekend and never came home." He'd asked her to go along on that trip, but she wasn't feeling well enough to make the hike to the cabin. It wasn't until after he'd left that a pregnancy test confirmed the reason for her fatigue and nausea. Lily was on her way. Tina had had big plans for springing the news when Thomas returned, but fate had other ones. "Two State Highway Patrol officers came to my door."

"I'm sorry," West said again, before she went any further. "I wish you hadn't had to go through that."

"Me, too."

When he glanced her way again there was curiosity on his brow. "How'd you meet him? If you don't mind me asking."

"It's okay," she said. "He spoke to me at the garden center a few days after I moved back here. I was buying redbud trees." A small smile touched her lips. "He helped me plant them in my backyard."

West grunted. His eyes narrowed, but he kept them focused on the road.

"I asked him once if he knew you," she said, feeling a little guilty for having asked one man in her life about another.

"And?"

"He laughed. He said he'd never had any reason to run into the sheriff."

"Lucky guy," West muttered.

Tina tried not to wonder if there was a dual meaning behind his words.

The pair rode in silence for several long blocks. West turned sharp blue eyes her way from time to time, rubbing the dark shadow of stubble on his cheeks without speaking.

"What?" she asked.

He shot her a small smile. "I shouldn't be surprised you've done so well despite it all. Remember that time you dared me to jump off that old rope into the swimming hole on New Year's Eve?"

"Like it was yesterday." She'd goaded West endlessly, daring and challenging him to be reckless, testing his stock. But West wasn't reckless, not even as a teen. He'd been the first man to show her they didn't all become monsters when the mood struck. West was as sensible as the day was long and a Garrett through and through. Hell-bent on saving the world. Garretts were soldiers and law enforcement officers. If rumor served, one of West's brothers was a federal agent and the other was a US marshal.

The cruiser took a slow turn into her neighborhood and stopped at the first crossroads. The rain had stopped, and muted sunlight streamed from behind thick gray clouds. Emerald green lawns stretched before them, lined in newly blooming mums and anchored in elaborate pumpkin arrangements showing off for Halloween. Lily was too small to know, but she was going to be a princess this year. Every year, if Tina had any say in it.

River Park had been an up-and-coming neighborhood when Tina was young. She'd stared through dirty school bus windows for years as classmates poured on and off with clean clothes and new shoes every fall, and she'd dreamed of living there. Now, the homes were older and in her price range as long as she budgeted. Lily would have safe streets to ride her bike on and neighbors who knew her name. Maybe even a few folks who cared where she went and who she was with.

"Here?" West asked at the next intersection.

"Two blocks up, on the left. The white farmhouse."

West accelerated to the posted speed limit. "I think you should see a doctor before we go to the station."

"No." She watched her unsuspecting neighborhood crawl past. Did the neighbors have any idea what had happened today? Was it on the news? Steven was dead. Pointlessly murdered by a coward with a gun. How did a community move on from that?

"I'll swing by the hospital on our way to the station. Better to be safe."

"No," she repeated, a little more forcefully this time. "I wasn't hurt, just shaken, and every minute counts right now. I want to be helpful."

West huffed, but didn't argue.

"Here. This one," Tina said as her little home came into view, all country with a wraparound porch and a tree in the front. "I won't be more than five minutes."

Confusion pinched her brow as Ducky, her golden retriever pup, jogged toward the car, tail flopping.

"You know that guy?" West asked, watching the happy dog outside his window.

"He's mine," Tina whispered, "but I left him in his crate when I went to work this morning." Her heart jammed into her throat, making it impossible to swallow. "Someone let him out."

THE CRUISER JERKED to a rocking stop. West was on his feet and striding toward her home a moment later. He notified Dispatch of a possible break-in, then unholstered his sidearm. A break-in and a shooting involving the same woman on the same morning wasn't a coincidence.

Tina was on his heels, teeth chattering intensely behind him.

He stopped her at the front door. "Wait in the car. Lock the doors."

"I can't."

The terror in her voice tugged his heart, and West weighed his options. Taking her along could be dangerous. Leaving her alone could be deadly. He turned the knob, and her door opened. "Stay behind me."

Her small fingers slid against the material over his back, and he hated the pleasure it gave him to be near her again.

Inside, the house was silent and spotless. "Cade County Sheriff," West announced, edging past about a hundred pairs of shoes by the front door.

"Woof!" Ducky called from Tina's side.

West reached around Tina and let the dog in.

Ducky barreled through the house, barking and protesting. He slid around a corner and out of sight.

West motioned for Tina to wait as he followed Ducky down a short hallway toward the back of the home. The dog stopped in the mudroom, pawing and barking at a narrow closet door.

"Cade County Sheriff," West announced again, stepping carefully into the small room. He moved into position, gun drawn and faced off with the door. "Come out with your hands up."

A blinding pain split the back of his head and loosened his grip on the weapon. Flashes of light splintered his vision. His knees buckled and he tumbled forward against his will. One palm landed against the floor in support.

The back door swung wide and a figure dressed in black bolted into the yard.

"Damn it." West shoved onto his feet and forced himself through the door. He slid in the wet grass on uncooperative legs. "Freeze!" he hollered.

A fresh blast of pain punched through his skull at the sound of his booming voice. He pressed one hand to the back of his head and groaned. The goose egg was already forming, and his palm slid against something warm and slick. A quick look confirmed the substance as his blood.

West angled between the next set of homes, hoping to get a glimpse of the getaway car or a look at the man's face. The figure had doubled the distance between them, clearing the next hill and vanishing before West could manage to gain any speed.

West holstered his sidearm and radioed Dispatch. "Suspect is fleeing on foot, moving southwest toward Main from River Park Estates." He'd be lucky if a deputy was anywhere near his location. The Cade County Sheriff's Department was small, just six including himself, and not everyone was on duty. Those who were had their hands full with the shooting.

He paused to curse and allow his vision to clear.

What the hell had he been hit with? And what was the dog barking at if not the intruder?

West climbed the steps to Tina's front porch slowly and with a little effort. "He got away," he said, sliding inside and forcing his posture straighter. "Got any ice?" He scanned the empty living room. "Tina?"

Ducky jumped at his feet, a leash in his mouth. "Now you want to go out?" He sidestepped Ducky and fought an irrational wave of fear. "Tina?"

"West." Her trembling voice sent him in the direction of her kitchen.

He cut through the living room, taking in as many details as possible. Everything smelled like Tina. Vanilla and cinnamon, warm and inviting. There wasn't much in the way of furniture, but the baby seemed to have more than any one child could ever need. Infant seats, swings and play sets dotted every inch of space he passed, accompanied by a barrel of stuffed animals in the living area.

Tina stood alone in the kitchen's center. The table had been set for two, complete with hot pads in the middle, as if standing in anticipation of a meal yet to come. She shook her head, clearly baffled. "I didn't do this."

West's muscles tightened. "Don't touch anything." He dialed Cole as an icy swell of fear rose through him. West knew exactly the kind of person who'd break into a woman's home and stage a scene like this. A dangerous one. Maybe even someone capable of shooting a man right in front of her just to get her attention. He turned away from Tina as he relayed the situation to his brother. The pain in his head grew by the second. West checked again to see if the blood flow had slowed.

Tina gathered ice into a dish towel and pushed it his way.

He gave her a sour face, but accepted the offer. "This is the opposite of not touching anything."

"Yeah, well, you're hurt," she said. "Don't bleed on my carpet." The attempt at levity was lost with the crack in her voice.

Tina was scared, and West needed to fix that.

He cleared the rest of the house, room by room, then took a break to let the ice do its work. "Any idea who'd pretend to make you dinner?" He winced as the towel slid against his hair.

"None."

"Are you seeing anyone?"

"No."

"I think you'd better pack a bag. I need to get a team out here to pull prints off the dog's crate, your doors and everything in the kitchen." He gripped the back of his neck. "As soon as they finish at the medical center parking lot."

Tina followed him into the bathroom and retrieved a first-aid kit from under the sink. "The house is clear. Now hold still and tell me what happened."

"Ducky was barking at the closet door, and someone jumped me while I was distracted."

The pup appeared at the sound of his name. *"Woof."*

Tina took the lead from his mouth and set it aside.

"We keep his leash in the closet. I take him for a walk when I get home."

West rolled his eyes and regretted it. "Ow."

"Here." She tossed a bloodied cloth into the sink and handed him a bottle of aspirin. "I don't think you'll need stitches."

"Great. I wasn't planning on getting any." He tossed a pair of pills into his mouth and scooped a handful of water from the bathroom sink.

He led her to her bedroom and made a slow circle through the room. "We know someone has been inside. We don't know for how long or how often." West peered through the curtains into the back and side yards. "Crimes like this are predominately orchestrated by men. Are you sure there isn't anyone you can think of who might have some fixation on you or infatuation you weren't aware of?" He ignored the fire burning in him at the thought. He couldn't let this get personal. Couldn't afford to have clouded judgment.

"I haven't dated since I met Thomas. That was two years ago. There was nothing serious before that."

West ignored the strike to his chest. He thought that they had been plenty serious once, but then again, she'd already made it clear he was wrong.

Tina wrinkled her nose. "There was a man at the hospital who asked me out a few times while I was pregnant. I thought that was weird, but he eventually took no for an answer."

"Who was that?"

"Chris something. He worked at the pharmacy on the main floor."

West released the curtains in favor of his cell phone. "Go ahead and gather whatever you need," he instructed, tapping the tiny screen. "You can shower and change at the station if you'd like. Your soiled clothes will need to be bagged as evidence. We can come back for Ducky once we finish there."

"How long will I be gone? How much should I pack?" Her mind raced with questions. Where should she and her daughter go? Was anywhere safe?

"Take enough to last you a couple days, Lily, too."

Tina braced her hands against the bed's edge. "Do you think the shooter did this?" Her ivory skin whitened further.

West sent a quick string of orders to his deputies via text message before turning his attention back to Tina. "We can't know for sure. Not yet."

"Was it him?" She choked. "Could the shooter from my office have been *here*? Inside my home?"

"That's what we're going to find out."

"Damn it, West!" A flush of frustration bled across her pale cheeks. "Stop dancing around and just tell me what you really think happened here."

West wedged his hands against his hips, struggling to deliver the impossible truth. As if playing witness to murder wasn't enough horror for her to experience today, the psychopath had to invade her home and do *who knew what* while she was trying to save the life of her patient. "I don't think this is a coincidence."

She nodded her head, an expression of disbelief on

her brow. "So, this is about me? The shooting, too? Steven died because of me somehow? It's insane! He'd barely begun his recovery." She stopped. "I think I'm going to be sick."

"You're probably in shock." West offered a hand to help her onto the bed. "Sit back. Put your head between your knees and breathe." He waited for her to comply. "You okay now?"

"No."

West turned to lean against the bed at her side. "None of the things that have happened today are your fault. None of them. Whoever's doing this is unstable. Deranged. He could've picked anyone to unleash his anger on. It had nothing to do with you. It could just as easily have been the neighbor, or the grocery clerk, or the librarian. Understand?"

She sobbed against the back of her hand, but nodded her agreement.

West stepped away from the bed. He needed to get her out of there. "Do you want me to pack the bag?"

Tina slid onto her feet. "Don't you ever get tired of bossing people around?" she grouched.

"No. Where are your bags?"

"Oh, my gosh! Lily!" She dug into her purse and brought out her phone. "I have to call the sitter. If this is about me, then Lily's in danger!"

West moved into her line of sight. "That's not a guarantee, and I've already sent a deputy to check on her."

"How did you know where she was?"

He smiled. "There's a giant pink heart on the refrigerator with Lily's schedule and Mary's contact information. I saw it when you got me the ice."

Her lips lifted into a small smile. "Right. Thank you." She adjusted the phone against her cheek. "Mary? This is Tina. How's Lily?" Tina's voice cracked on the last little word. Tears rolled over her cheeks as her smile widened and turned to laughter. "Thank you. Okay. Thank you." When she disconnected, Tina looked weightless, as if everything awful in her day had been forgotten. "Lily's okay. Mary saw what happened on the news. She's been worried about me, but they're both fine. They're eating applesauce and blowing bubbles. She said I should take as long as I need. She knows I have things to sort out, but I just want to end this awful day and pick up my baby. The sooner I have her back in my arms, the sooner something might make sense again."

She stuffed her things into a bag from the closet then looked at the bathroom door. "Should I bring a towel for the shower?"

"No." West marveled at the way the promise of seeing her baby had rejuvenated and refocused her. "We have towels at the station."

"Okay." Tina rolled her shoulders back and hiked the bag over one shoulder. "Let me grab Lily's things, and we can go."

Chapter Three

Tina touched her hair nervously as she entered the bustling sheriff's department. West hadn't made a big deal out of her appearance, but she knew exactly what she looked like. Death.

The cluster of deputies and administrative staff huddled around a desk straightened to welcome their leader. Cole broke away from the group as West and Tina approached. The others stopped to stare.

"Tina Ellet," West said, "I'd like you to meet the Cade County Sheriff's Department. Team, this is Miss Ellet."

The group offered warm smiles, but their gazes traveled the circuit from her to West and then to Cole. He'd clearly filled the group in on her history with their sheriff. Ridiculously, her cheeks heated.

Cole greeted West with a handshake, then turned an apologetic expression on Tina. "I'm sorry this is happening to you." He barely resembled the gangly teen she remembered. No more acne or braces. His undeniable Garrett genes had brought him through puberty with a gold star. Exactly like his brothers.

She pulled the bag higher on her shoulder and gripped it with one hand. "Thanks."

Tina scanned her new surroundings with curiosity. Miraculously, she'd never been inside the station before. It wasn't the way she'd imagined. Based on the horror stories her father had told, she'd assumed the place was dark and scary. Full of people like him in handcuffs. Instead, the building was open-concept, bright and clean. The walls were lined in diplomas, Don't Text and Drive posters and a cluster of community boards with fund-raising flyers pinned to them.

West lifted a hand in Tina's direction, but dropped it quickly with a frown. "There's coffee and hot water for tea in the break room, and there's normally something to eat on the counter. Fruit. Bagels." He stepped away from the little group, and she followed.

She hurried behind him down a long hallway lined with closed doors. Her stomach twisted into painful knots at the thought of food. "Just a shower, I think."

He stopped at a door marked Locker Room. "We'll need to put your clothes into an evidence bag, so leave them out when you're done." He pushed the door open and held it for her. "I'll flip the in-use sign so no one bothers you. Small building. Everything's coed."

Tina hesitated. Police station or not, the empty room was frightening. "Will you be here when I get out?"

West looked over his shoulder. "I'll try. I need to touch base with my team and see what's been done. If no one's visited the two men who missed your group this afternoon, then I'd like to get over there myself.

I've got a limited number of deputies and a vested interest in this case."

Tina tried not to wonder if that "vested interest" was her. "Has anyone tried calling the men who missed the meeting?" Why hadn't she thought to do that? "I have their numbers in my phone." She dug nervously through the giant bag on her shoulder and nearly dumped the contents.

"Hey." West's steady hand fell upon her fluttering one. "Stop." He gripped her fingers until she looked his way.

She pulled in deep breaths, borrowing strength from his touch. "What if the gunman visited them before coming to our session? Maybe that's why they weren't in group today."

"It's unlikely," West said, "but we're going to find out. Plus, I have questions for them. We really don't know what's going on in the big picture yet." He lowered his face to her level and searched her with kind eyes. "Can you think of any connection between the victim and yourself beyond your recent professional relationship?"

Tina considered the way she'd found Steven asleep at a bus stop outside the hospital last month. They were strangers until then, and had only seen each other at group sessions since. "No. None. Why?"

"I'm still trying to figure out how the shooting and the break-in are related. The crimes are vastly different, but the timing has my flags up. If the shooter is the same man who attacked me at your home, understanding the link between the three of you would be helpful. I'll be back once I drop in on your absentees, then we can finish our interview. I still need a formal statement from you."

Tina straightened. "Take me with you."

He followed her lead, returning to his full height with a snap. "I don't think that's a good idea."

"West."

His expression changed, ever so slightly.

"Please." The stubborn sting of emotion bit at her eyes and nose. "I need to know the rest of my patients are safe. If they don't answer their phones, I'm going to pay them visits myself. Seems like I'd be safer with you."

"I need you here making a formal statement."

"I'll write it while you drive. I promise." She hoped the desperation in her heart came through in her tone. "Please don't leave me behind."

West ducked his head and gripped the back of his neck. "You shower. I'll try to reach the men by phone before I leave. We already have their numbers." He turned on his heels and walked away.

"Does that mean I can go with you?" she called after him.

"You've got ten minutes."

Tina ran for the shower. Ten minutes wouldn't have seemed like long enough time to get wet before Lily was born. Since then, Tina had learned to do almost anything in a quarter of the time it had once taken.

She folded her stained clothes and stacked them on a bench for evidence, tucking her underthings carefully between the pieces, unsure if she was meant to turn those in, too. These were things a person should never have to wonder. The things that had happened today didn't belong in Shadow Point, Kentucky. They were fodder for television crime shows or the headlines of a city she'd never visit.

Tina doused her hair with shampoo and lathered her body fron neck to toes in seconds, scrubbing harder than necessary, until the water ran clear. Ironic, because she doubted the stains from her day would ever truly be gone. She shook off the heavy wave of emotion and concentrated on the ticking clock. The damp towel was in the communal hamper and she was re-dressed with four minutes to spare. Tina grabbed her things and yanked open the locker room door. Hopefully, West had really waited. If he hadn't, she wouldn't blame him.

She'd always hated the way she'd left things with him after high school. When the college scholarship she'd applied for came through, she'd packed up and asked him to understand. It wasn't an opportunity anyone could pass up, certainly not her. She'd needed to get out of Shadow Point like she needed oxygen. West had wanted to get married. He'd wanted a house and some land, a perfect replica of what his parents had, but Tina didn't believe in fairy tales, and at eighteen, she couldn't see past her escape. She'd picked up the phone a thousand times over the years to tell him the truth about why she had to leave. Her family was a train wreck. Her father was in jail now, probably for the rest of his life, and her mother had run away in his absence. Tina was broken because of it, and West deserved better. Without her to hold him back, West had enlisted in the military, served overseas and come home to be the county sheriff. She had been baggage for him, but she could never find the strength to say those things out loud, so she didn't. Pride was vindictive that way.

WEST PRESSED HIS palms to the desk, scanning the map before him. Cole and the other Cade County deputies had compiled a list of viable reports about a man in a dark jacket and jeans spotted near the crime scene. Though no one outside Tina's group had witnessed the attack, several had heard the gunshot and called to report it. A handful had confirmed Tina's claim about the old pickup truck. "You can't throw a stone without hitting an old pickup in this county," West groaned.

"Someone thought it was a faded red Ford," Cole said. "That's something."

West rubbed his eyes. Let Cole be the optimist for a change. Someone had to be because West wasn't finding a lot of hope in the reports he had in front of him. The descriptions were in agreement, but the locations were all over the place. "So he either went north or south?"

Cole sighed. "Yep."

West strained upright and shook his head. "Did we catch a lead on the assailant at Tina's home?"

"No." Cole lifted his brows. "How's your head?"

West frowned. "Hurts. What else do you have for me?"

"We found a standard 30-06 shell casing on the building's roof at the crime scene."

"I guess that's something."

Cole didn't look hopeful. "It's the same ammo we'd find in half the homes in Cade County. Hell, I've got the same stuff at my place."

West adjusted his hat over the tender lump. If Cole saw it, he'd try to administer first aid, and he'd had enough of that from Tina. "See if ballistics can get a match. Maybe the gun's been used in another crime. We might be able to find him that way." He pulled his shoulders back, trying and failing to alleviate the tension there. "Have we been able to reach either missing group member?"

Cole pressed his lips and shook his head. "No. When I couldn't reach them at their home numbers, I called their places of employment. One man went to work on schedule last night and left this morning without incident. The other called off before breakfast."

West grabbed his keys. "So, both whereabouts are unaccounted for. I'm heading out to see what kept them away from the meeting. Let Tina know—"

"Let Tina know what?" Her voice startled him into a spin. "By my watch, I have two minutes left on the ten you gave me."

Cole smiled against one fist, then failed to cover his humor with a cough. "You want to split the work, boss? I'll hit one, you take the other?"

"I'd like to speak with them both," Tina said.

Cole cast a quizzical look in West's direction.

West shook his head. "Why don't you take the guy who went to work last night? I'll take the guy who called off this morning."

Cole ducked his chin and made for the door.

West turned to address the remaining deputies. "Call me direct with anything new. I want to be kept up to the minute on this, and when they're done collecting prints over at Miss Ellet's home, have someone stay put until I get back."

A round of "Yes, sirs" drifted through the electrified air. West's chest puffed with pride. His deputies were the best in the state. He'd made a habit of reaching out to the most dedicated and promising rookies as early as possible, and when positions arose within his team, he gave those men and women a call. It was a practice he'd learned from his father, the sheriff before him. Stacking the deck in Cade County's favor was a Garrett family tradition, and one more reason the son of a gun who did this would soon be sorry.

He shoved the front door open and held it for Tina to pass.

She stopped to face him in the narrow threshold. "You were going to leave me?" Her steel blue eyes nailed him to the wall.

West swallowed long and slow. The energy building between them in the small space was more of a distraction than he could allow. A fitted sweater and jeans clung to her youthful figure, reminding him of the many times he'd personally helped her out of them. He extended one arm into the dreary day. "You're here now, so let's go."

THE RIDE TO Carl Morgan's house was long and slow. The heater vents circulated scents of Tina's shampoo and perfume around his head in a hurricane of distraction. "Tell me about this guy," West said, flipping his headlights on to illuminate the gloomy road.

Tina shifted in her seat, angling toward him. "Carl's a nice man. He's about our age, originally from Florida. He works at Franklin's Garage. Lives alone. He's quiet and a little detached. It's common with trauma survivors. Tender hearts hurt deeply, and we live in a world where growing tough skin is practically a survival requirement."

"Could he have gotten himself into trouble? Maybe ticked off a homicidal maniac?"

Tina's head was shaking before West stopped talking. "No. Carl's a people-pleaser, but he'd avoid intimidating individuals."

"Not every shooter is an intimidating individual. Look at school shooters and others who've committed similar crimes. They're a lot of things, but dangerous-looking isn't one of them."

She glanced his way, then back at the road.

"Given that you are well aware of the profile for someone who'd pull a stunt like this, can you tell me unequivocally that neither Carl Morgan or Tucker Bixby fit the mold?"

"No, but I can tell you there isn't a mold, and that the number of patients in therapy is far smaller than the number of folks who need it but aren't getting it. There are probably a hundred people in Cade County who psychologically fit the bill that we don't know about. So you have no hard evidence to support your theory that the shooter is connected to my group."

West gripped the wheel tighter, unable to argue and unwilling to upset her further by playing devil's advocate. The truth was, he had no idea what was going on in his county today. "Is there anything else you can tell me about Carl before we get there?"

"No. Just that he's doing phenomenally in group, so please don't upset him if you can help it. News of the shooting will be tough enough—badgering him could set his progress back, and I don't want that."

The country road rose and fell before them under a covering of gray clouds. Green reflections of little eyes blinked along the roadside, considering a test of their fate.

It was late in October and nearing lunchtime already. Barely six hours of sunlight remaining. West had enjoyed autumn as a kid, but he'd learned to see it as a hindrance after joining local law enforcement. Shorter days meant fewer hours to look for clues and missing people. It also gave criminals more time to hide under the cover of night.

Tina fidgeted with the hem of her sweater. "Where do you think the shooter is now? Do people like that just go home and have dinner? Do they kill themselves? Leave the state?"

"Depends." West slowed the cruiser to a crawl at the end of a narrow dirt road. Peeling numbers on the battered mailbox suggested that they'd arrived. "This it?"

"I don't know. I've never been here."

West spun his wheel, navigating a sharp right into the unknown. No Trespassing signs were nailed to posts on either side of the road. A trailer stood fifty feet back, bookended by trees and a picnic table. An aged blue car sat in a bed of gravel out front.

"That's his car," Tina said, unbuckling her belt.

"Wait." West stretched a hand across her middle like a guard gate. "It's dark under all these clouds and trees. I want you to stay put until I give you a signal."

"Why?" She dropped her voice to a low, ragged whisper. "Do you think the killer's here?"

He gave the dark trailer another long inspection. "Not necessarily. There's only one vehicle, and it's not a pickup, but I'd rather be safe, so wait here until I give you an all clear. Understand?"

"Okay."

He popped his door open and flashed her a warning look when the interior light came on. "I mean it this time."

She made a show of fixing her hands on her lap.

West flipped his bright lights on and locked her in the car. The cruiser's headlights illuminated a path to the trailer. West scanned the ground for signs of a struggle as he moved. Nothing unusual, no fallen items, drag marks or drops of blood. He stepped with care onto the makeshift wooden deck outside the front door, and a motion light snapped on.

West's heart rate sprang into overdrive. He re-seated his sidearm, unleashed on instinct at the unexpected flick of the light, and rapped on the trailer door. Surprisingly, the shock hadn't increased his headache. The aspirin must've finally taken effect. He braced his free palm against the butt of his gun. "Cade County Sheriff, Mr. Morgan," he boomed.

The trailer rocked slightly. Interior lights flashed on one by one from the back to the front. West moved away as the silver door swung open.

A heavy-lidded man in worn jeans and a faded blue T-shirt squinted at the cruiser's lights. "Hello?"

"Over here, Mr. Morgan," West said. "Do you know why I'm here?" He examined Carl slowly for signs of a weapon.

Carl blinked long and slow, scrubbing calloused hands over his thick brown hair. "Was there an accident on the road?"

"No, sir." West took a more relaxed stance, but kept the distance. "You want to tell me why you aren't at work?"

"I had a migraine." He pressed a palm to one side of his head in evidence. "I've been in bed."

"You get migraines often?"

"Sometimes." Carl's gaze drifted back to the cruiser. "Is someone else in there?" He shielded his eyes with one hand.

West ignored the question. "You've been home all morning?"

Carl dipped his chin, still preoccupied with the cruiser's lights.

"Any visitors?"

"Not until you. Why? I don't understand what's going on."

"You missed your group session. Don't you usually call ahead if you're not coming?"

"I—I've never missed. I d-didn't know I had to call."

The stutter gave West pause. Tina's words came back to mind. Much as he'd like to continue questioning Carl alone, he didn't want to be the reason the man relapsed or whatever Tina had just warned might happen. He lifted a hand without taking his eyes off Carl and opened and shut his palm, beckoning Tina from her place of safety. He changed positions as she approached, putting the trailer's wall at his back and everything else within his line of vision, peripheral or otherwise.

The passenger door opened, and Carl took a step backward, arm extended toward the trailer door.

"Stop," West ordered, and both people froze. He motioned to Tina again, attention fixed on Carl. "Keep your hands where I can see them, Mr. Morgan."

He didn't have to guess when Tina came into focus for Carl. The man's eyebrows stretched into his hairline, and his mouth dropped open. It was the reaction he expected most men had when they first saw her. Having been the onetime recipient of her rejection, West might've felt bad for the guy if there wasn't a shooter in town with his sick mind set on Tina. As far as West was concerned, all men were suspects until proven otherwise.

Chapter Four

"Hi, Carl." Tina spoke carefully as she climbed onto the wooden platform outside the trailer. Water dripped from the ragged awning stretched overhead, remnant drops from the recent storm. "I missed you at group today."

Carl's eyes darted between her, the headlights and the brooding sheriff at his side. "I—I'm a little surprised you felt the offense required an intervention by l-law enf-f-forcement." His expression softened with the joke.

Tina smiled, thankful to see Carl at ease. She flicked West a meaningful look. "Maybe we can cut the spotlight."

West leveled Carl with a no-nonsense expression before finally stepping away.

Carl moved closer to Tina the instant West abandoned his position as watchdog. "This isn't really about me. Is it?"

"Not at all." Tina shook her head, hoping to look less on edge than she felt.

"Are you okay?" Carl asked. "Did something happen to you? To Lily? Is there anything I can do? If you need a place to stay, I—I have plenty of room."

"No. Nothing like that, exactly. Something happened after group today, and we wanted to check on you. Make sure you were okay."

His mouth curved into a small smile. "You were worried about m-me?"

"Yeah." Memories of the moments outside her office flashed back to mind, stinging her eyes and drying her mouth.

The blinding headlights extinguished, and Tina blinked several times to readjust her vision. "There was a shooting."

West returned to them slowly, watching with careful cop eyes, one hand resting on the butt of his gun. Tina doubted that he missed much as town sheriff. He'd missed very little as a teen. She could only imagine his power of perception had grown keener with training and maturity.

Carl's gaze traveled quizzically over Tina. "You weren't hurt."

"No. Not me."

West shifted his weight, drawing Carl's attention. "Another member of your group was murdered today. Steven Masters. How well did you know him?"

Tina narrowed her eyes on West. He could've been a little tactful about announcing a person's death.

Something in his expression said he'd been intentionally harsh. Too much tightness in his jaw and rigidity in his stance. West didn't trust Carl. Why?

Carl pointedly ignored him. "I only kn-kn-knew Steven from gr-gr-group."

"You don't seem too choked up," West said.

"I guess I'm stun-stun-stunned."

Cold wind whipped through the trees and rattled the tattered awning over their heads. West was right. Carl didn't seem to care at all. She fell back a half step. Did it truly not matter to him that a man he knew was murdered, or hadn't the shock registered yet?

Carl stepped closer, erasing the bit of distance she'd created. "Are you cold? Do you need a c-coat?"

"No. I'm fine. We're here to check on you."

"Yeah, but this must b-be awful for you." He angled his back to West. "You and Steven were getting p-p-pretty close."

"How so?" West asked, moving into the space at Tina's side and blatantly hovering over her patient.

Carl stiffened. "They spent extra time together before and after sessions. She does that with new members." He touched Tina's sleeve gently. "If you n-need someone to talk to…"

Tina wrapped shaky arms around her center and attempted to stifle her recoil. How well did she know the members of her group? Could one of them truly be a killer? Could Carl? "Thank you. I'm sure this is something we'll be talking about for months to come at our sessions."

His eyebrows tented and he shoved both hands deep into his pockets. A flicker of something dark flashed in his eyes, and Carl's suddenly heated expression fell on West. "I'm still not sure why you're here. I wasn't at group today, s-so I can't give a statement."

"Carl," Tina started softly, "can you think of anyone who'd want to hurt Steven? The shooter only took one shot. I've seen the two of you talking before. Did he tell you about anyone who was upset or holding a grudge against him?"

"No."

West sucked his teeth and continued to eyeball Carl. "Can anyone verify your whereabouts between seven and nine this morning?"

"No." Carl grinned. "I've been here all day." He opened his arms, as if to showcase the trees and silence around them.

"Is that right?" West asked. "My deputies tried calling. You didn't answer."

"I had a m-migraine. The ringer was off."

Tina's phone buzzed with Mary's signature tone. She peeked at the incoming message. A photo of Lily wearing a fancy hat with feathers and the caption *Playing dress up.*

Her eyes teared at the sight of her daughter's bright, toothless smile. The day had been too dark. She needed to cuddle Lily against her chest, inhale her sweet scent and feel her strong little heart beating against her own. Tina had told West that she wanted to visit both Carl and Tucker, but now she just wanted to be with her baby girl.

West pulled a buzzing phone from his pocket and barked a few monosyllables into the receiver, startling her from her thoughts.

"Carl—" Tina shot him a pleading look "—can you think of anything that might help us find the person who did this?"

"No."

"Okay." She nodded her acceptance. "I'll arrange a new location for next week's meeting while we all work through this loss. We'll talk more then."

West stretched his hand out to Carl, a business card stuck between his fingertips, cell phone put away. "Thank you for your time, Mr. Morgan." He caught Tina's hand in his. "If you think of anything that might be useful, give me a call."

Carl fixed his attention on West's hand over Tina's. "Will d-do."

Tina turned for the cruiser, thankful for the escape. She wasn't cut out for questioning people as if they were criminals. And Carl's response to her news wasn't at all what she'd expected. It left her feeling confused and uneasy. She could only hope his apparent indifference was a result of shock and not something far more gruesome.

WEST KEPT HIS eyes on Carl as he closed the passenger door for Tina, shutting her safely inside. The fragile and uncertain man she'd described wasn't the one who stood outside the trailer. His smooth transition between hostility toward West and concern for Tina set off all West's internal alarms. Not to mention how precisely his behavior had mimicked the day's crimes. A cold-blooded murder outside the medical complex, and a thoughtfully planned meal at Tina's home.

West folded himself behind the wheel and radioed their position to Dispatch.

He reversed down the gravel drive and pulled onto the country road, making plans to run a thorough background check on Mr. Morgan.

"Was that phone call back at the trailer more bad news?" Tina asked. "Did something else happen?"

"No. That was one of my deputies. Mary and Lily are doing fine. He's patrolling the neighborhood until you can get there, making a circuit and keeping watch on the streets around her home. If you don't see him when you arrive to pick Lily up, wait for him. He'll be back on his next loop, then he can follow you to your place and wait while you get Ducky."

Tina nodded slowly. "Will the deputy stay with me until I decide where to go? How much time do I have to decide?"

"I asked him to process your home while he's there, so you can take a minute to breathe, but limit the number of things you touch. I'm hoping he can get a good print from that dinner setup in the kitchen. My other men are finishing up at the medical complex, then following leads on the shooter and faded red pickup seen leaving the scene. Tucker Bixby wasn't home when Cole got there, so Cole's looking into his whereabouts. I imagine you'd like to get to your daughter now."

Tina blew out a long, labored breath. "Yes. Very much."

"I'll take you back to your car now," West said.

He fished a handkerchief from his pocket and passed it her way.

She accepted the offering and pressed it to the corner of each eye. She twisted the thin white fabric in her hands. "I can't believe you still carry this."

"Grandpa's handkerchief? We all do. I'm a little surprised you remember it."

Tina rolled wide eyes in his direction. "I remember that funeral like it was my own grandfather's. I remember each of your brothers with these hankies in their jacket pockets. Four brokenhearted pallbearers." She balled the fabric in one hand. "Hundreds of people came that day and filled every moment with love and kindness." She swiped a tear off her cheek. "It was beautiful. He would've been so proud."

"I'm sure he was." West turned his face to the road. "Grandpa told us regularly how important it was to build relationships. He touched a lot of lives." Next to his father, West's grandfather was the best man he'd ever known. His brothers and uncles came in a tight cluster for third. Love, pride and honor were always on tap at the Garrett house. "You okay?"

"I will be."

He tapped his thumbs against the steering wheel. "I hate to push this, but I still need a formal statement. You promised to write it while we were en route, and we're nearly back to your car."

Tina pulled the notepad and pen from her purse and began to write. Tears fell in fat drops onto the page as she worked.

West kept his mouth shut as long as possible, but he

hated seeing her cry. "How did you feel that interview with Carl went?" he asked. "Is he always so…" What was the word? She surely wouldn't approve of *creepy*.

She wiped the wet paper with his hanky. "I don't know."

"Based on your description before we got there, I'd expected a television-grade nerd or a little harmless guy afraid to make eye contact." Not the lean and borderline hostile man who'd answered the door.

"Whose fault is that?"

He ignored the question. West had heard it from her before, and the answer was always *West's*. Making assumptions might not have been his best attribute, but as a sheriff the practice had proven indispensable more times than he could count. "Do you think he had a problem with you spending extra time with Steven?"

"No. That's standard practice. Carl's been with the group long enough to know that."

"Do all the members have the same problems?"

Tina shot him a knowing look. She'd already made it clear she wouldn't divulge her patients' personal information. "They're all dealing with PTSD and severe emotional trauma for various reasons. Some members are former military. Some are abuse survivors."

"How did you spend the extra time you had with Steven?"

Tina sighed. "Occasionally I'd use the time to educate and encourage. Other times, he'd tell me things he wasn't ready to share with the group. It was all very up-and-up."

West repositioned his grip on the wheel, relaxing

his hands and leaning back against the seat. "I didn't mean to imply otherwise."

"You didn't. I just want it stated for the record."

He cocked a brow. "This isn't going on a record. We're just two old friends talking."

She turned her face to his, a sad smile on her full pink lips. "Is that what we are, West?"

"I'm not sure what we are now," he admitted, "but I was engaged once to a girl who looked a lot like you."

She dropped her gaze to the handkerchief briefly before pinning him with a powerful stare. "I'm not that girl anymore."

"No," he agreed. "Clearly, that girl has been upgraded by time and experience." He reached across the seat to give her knee a playful push. "I think the girl I knew would be proud."

A smile bloomed on her lips. "Thank you for saying that."

"I meant it."

She caught his fingers in hers and squeezed. "I know."

West released her to pull his cruiser into the lot outside her office.

The crime scene was roped off now, and two members of his team worked their way through a rain-soaked lot, careful not to miss anything that might lead them to the shooter's identity. Plastic yellow tee-pees with bold black numbers anchored the shattered glass and polka-dotted the surrounding area.

Tina shuddered beside him.

"I'll be by to check on you and Lily as soon as

I can, but I'm going to pay the hospital pharmacist a visit now." The one who'd asked her out multiple times during her pregnancy. "What did you say his name was?"

"Chris."

West itched to tighten his fingers around hers once more, but he wasn't sure how many times he could force himself to let go.

Tina rolled her head against the back of the seat, turning sharp blue eyes on him. "Tell me this wasn't because someone thought I was spending too much extra time with Steven." Her body tipped slightly toward his. The change was small, nearly imperceptible. So much so, Tina probably didn't even realize. But West did.

He felt the too-familiar pull at his core, an urge to meet her in the middle.

No amount of time would change that about them. He and Tina were human magnets in need of connection. Being near her without being *hers* was a new and ugly sensation. He didn't like it.

West cleared his throat. "We'll know more soon." His thoughts drifted back to Carl Morgan. The timing of Carl's absence with the shooting today was highly suspicious, and West didn't like the way Carl had looked at Tina. Definitely not the way a patient should look at his therapist, and it had taken all of West's self-control not to smack Carl's grubby hand away when he'd reached for her arm. The look in Carl's eyes when she recoiled was satisfying, but delivering the weirdo a solid right hook would've been even better. "We'll see what my team turns up and what Tucker and Chris have to say once we find them. We've got to follow the facts." Lucky for Carl, being creepy wasn't against the law, and West's gut instinct wasn't grounds to hold him.

Tina rolled her eyes, instantly looking a decade younger. She nudged his arm with a grin. "You still do that, huh? Answer my questions with random truths when you don't want to lie or upset me with the one I'm asking for."

Her hand lingered on his arm, warming him to the core.

West fought a budding smile. "Would you prefer I lie?"

"As if you could." She cracked the door open and swung her legs into the brisk autumn wind.

He circled the car and met her halfway to hers, toting the bags she'd packed at home earlier. "Slow down." He caught her wrist in his fingers, cursing himself instantly for the thrill it gave him. "Hey. Take a minute before you drive. You've had one hell of a day. You're worried about your baby, your safety, your group."

She stopped to face him. Her shoulders drooped. "I'm okay to drive."

"Okay, then tell me you have a plan before you shoot out of here. If you're planning to get a hotel room, you'd better change cars and register in cash under a different name. I'm going to need your contact information regardless, in case we have reason to believe you're in danger."

Her face went slack. "Maybe I could take Lily to Disneyland for a week. Or the beach. We can go somewhere far away for a while."

"Maybe." He'd like to think he'd have the son of a gun behind bars before dawn, but the odds certainly weren't in his favor, and he couldn't promise he'd have him caught in a week, either. "How long can you afford something like that?"

"I don't know." Her voice ratcheted an octave as fear changed her expression to something panicked and feral. "I've never been stalked, or hunted, or anything like this before, if that's even what this is. You're the expert. What are we supposed to do?"

West couldn't give her an answer. He didn't have one.

He ached to fold her into his arms and kiss her head like he used to. He wanted to fix this. All of this. He'd never wanted anything more than to keep her safe and make her smile. And ten years apart hadn't changed a damn thing.

Tina groaned and rubbed her eyes. "I need coffee. I need to fix my face, paste on a smile and make sure Lily doesn't pick up on any of the horrific things rolling through my head."

She pried her keys from her handbag and beeped her car doors unlocked. "I'll get Lily and Ducky, then I'll figure out where we're going before your deputy leaves my place. I'll call you as soon as I know."

He shifted his weight. "I'll head over to your house as soon as I can." He passed her the bags, and she tossed them onto her passenger seat.

Tina slid her hand down the length of West's arm, catching his fingers in hers. "I'm glad you're here."

"Always," he said, returning the gentle squeeze.

They stood in palpable silence for a long moment, evaluating one another, it seemed. There was obviously something more Tina wanted to say.

She didn't.

Instead, she dropped behind the wheel of her car and motored away.

They were beginning to make a bad habit of this.

Her leaving, and him watching helplessly from behind.

Chapter Five

Tina turned onto the main road with a sigh of relief, thankful to put a little distance between herself and the man causing her already shocked and broken heart so much unnecessary confusion. She dialed Mary and set the phone to speaker.

Thankfully, the call connected on the first ring. "Hi, Tina," Mary answered. "How are you? Is everything okay?"

Tina checked her mirrors and adjusted her defrost vents. "I've been better. How are you and Lily?"

"Lily's sound asleep, and a strapping young deputy is patrolling my neighborhood, so I'm not doing too bad, either."

"Great." A smile edged over Tina's lips. Mary was Tina's first friend after moving back to town. She wasn't much older than Tina's mom, and she missed caring for children, so the arrangement with Lily was perfect all around. "Well, I'm finally on my way. Can I bring you anything?"

"You don't need to do that. You've had an awful day. Besides, Lily and I ate lunch before she went to sleep." Mary gave a sad laugh. "Considering what you've been through, I should probably be making you lunch." She paused. "Do you want me to make you lunch? Maybe pour you a glass of wine? I'm a great listener if you need someone to talk to."

"No." Tina almost laughed. She didn't drink, and it was barely past noon, but after the morning she'd had a glass of wine didn't sound half bad. "How about I buy you a fancy coffee instead? Cup of Life is on the way to your place from here."

"Fine," Mary agreed. "I will accept your coffee, but only if you agree to stay a few minutes before you take off again. I worry about you. Sometimes I think you get so busy taking care of everyone else that you forget to take care of yourself."

Tina didn't have the energy to argue or confess all that had happened today. Like the possibility she may have been the reason for Steven's death. Or that, even if she wasn't, someone had still been in her home. Touched her things. Pretended to make her dinner.

An involuntary shiver coursed down her back. "I've got to go. I'll see you soon."

Tina disconnected, then loosened her grip on the wheel, bending and stretching her fingers in a futile attempt to relax. She needed a better headspace before holding her baby again. Lily was sure to pick up on the anxiety pouring off her mother in buckets.

Tina closed her eyes at the red light, and West's deceptively gruff image appeared. She popped her lids open and cursed herself internally. Given all that had transpired today, it was ludicrous she couldn't concentrate on anything but memories of his determined face.

She eased her foot off the brake as the light turned green.

She'd been back in town for nearly two years, and had managed to date, get married and have a baby, all without running into a single Garrett. Now, after just a few hours at his side, she was seventeen all over again, wondering when she would see him next, and if his heart still beat as fast as hers when they touched. More important, could he forgive her for the way she'd left things between them all those years ago?

West's opinion of her had always mattered. As much today as it had when they were young and wildly in love. She groaned inwardly at the thought. It had been unfair for her to let him love her then. Back when she had been a lie. She'd put up a nice show. Smoke and mirrors to distract from what she really was. He gave her his all, but she'd never really let him in. She'd kept the real things to herself.

She'd known what people said about her, of course. She fed on the gossip, imagining her life was something other than it was, letting people believe anything, so long as it wasn't the truth. She'd pretended to be rail thin by choice, instead of half starved, pretended to wear too-short shorts for attention, when the truth was that she kept getting taller, and clothes were expensive.

No more.

Now, she had a stack of jeans in her closet, all the right size, and Lily had more clothes than one child could ever want, whatever the season. Tina would never be that helpless child again, and her daughter would never know the humiliation of a life without a mother's love.

Possibly the only thing she loved more than knowing how much she had changed was knowing that West hadn't changed at all. He was still strong and certain, reliable and steadfast. All the things she'd fallen in love with long ago. Even being with him again for a short time had made her miss the family she never had and long for a husband to cradle their daughter. She wanted someone she could find strength in when hers was gone.

The coffee shop came into view, and Tina shook off the useless thoughts and childish fantasies. She pulled up to the window at Cup of Life and freed some money from her wallet. "I'll take two medium lattes, please. And I'd like to pay for the car behind me."

Tina inched forward, waiting her turn, but eager to get moving once more. She traded cash for coffee and waved in her rearview mirror at the couple behind her who was about to get a nice surprise. Paying for the next person in line was something Tina had done throughout her adult life. It was an act of kindness that someone had performed for her family on a night they'd planned to dine and ditch because there wasn't enough money for food, and they hadn't eaten in two days. It didn't seem logical, but there were tougher things than living with an alcoholic father and depressive mother. Consistently going hungry was one of them.

Mary's house came quickly into view from there. Only three short blocks from Cup of Life, nestled in a mostly rural neighborhood with more livestock than people. Electric candles burned in the windows, but the porch light was off.

Rolling thunder growled in the distance as Tina shifted into Park and squinted at the darkened doorstep. Maybe it was the day she was having, but something felt off. Instinct crawled over her skin like a nest of baby spiders, and she worked to pull herself together. There was no need to worry Mary any further or upset her sweet daughter.

It's fine, she told herself, *just breathe*.

She shored her resolve and palmed her keys.

A massive bolt of lightning slashed the gray sky, illuminating Mary's open front door before dropping the house back into darkness.

A block of fear lodged in Tina's throat. She fumbled for her phone, dialing West as she flung off her seat belt. Her car door jerked open with help from the raging wind, and she lunged into a sprint.

"Sheriff Garrett," West's voice boomed through the receiver at Tina's ear.

"West. I'm at Mary's house and the front door is open. Everything is dark." She took the porch steps two at a time.

"Mary! Lily!" she called, praying this wasn't what it seemed. Anything but a crime involving her daughter.

"Go back to your car and lock the doors," West

ordered. An engine growled through the speaker at Tina's ear. "I'm on my way. I'm notifying Dispatch. Do not leave the car for any reason, and do not hang up."

"My baby..." She leapt across the threshold, blindly smacking the wall beside her in search of light switches, unable to voice the horrific and blood-curdling things that raced through her mind. "Mary!"

"Be careful," West growled. "You need to slow down and think. This could be a trap."

"I don't give a damn, West Garrett!" she screamed. "I need to find my daughter!"

Tina sprinted through the old farmhouse toward the room where Lily normally slept, sliding over hardwood floors and knocking into walls as she took the corners at full speed.

She clutched the stairwell and used the spindles to propel her faster than her feet alone could move her onto the second floor. "Lily!" She'd give anything to hear that sweet cry. Anything to know she was safe in the crib where Mary had laid her. Hot tears rolled over her cheeks as she tore down the silent hallway, toward the dark room with the open door at the end. Images of tiny pink lambs and clouds floated dreamily over the walls and ceiling, cast from a domed night-light.

She came to a stop in the room's center. Her collapsing heart nearly dropping her onto the floor. The crib was empty. "She's not here." The words clawed their way free from her tightening throat.

"And Mary?" West asked.

"I don't know." Tina stumbled from the room, gasping for air through a tightening chest. One by one she checked the rooms for a sign of her friend and babysitter. Maybe Mary had taken Lily someplace safe. Maybe they were hiding together.

"I'm just five minutes away now," West said. "The deputy patrolling her neighborhood should be back any minute. He'll handle things until I get there. Please go back to your car."

"I can't," she cried. "What if they're here? What if they're hurt?" Tina flung open closet doors and screamed until her throat burned raw.

She slid to a halt in the first-floor mudroom, heart hammering and stomach twisting.

Mary lay sprawled on the floor, hands outstretched toward the wide-open back door.

Tina screamed until black dots raged in her periphery and the world slanted beneath her.

WEST ARRIVED MINUTES LATER, having listened to the silence for far too long. It was as if Tina had died on the spot after delivering that scream. He'd soundly broken every traffic law on record to get there from Tucker's neighborhood, where he'd rendezvoused with Cole to knock on doors. Neighbors confirmed that Tucker hadn't been home since the night before. West hadn't even had time to visit Chris, the questionable pharmacist.

He crammed the gearshift into Park and jumped

free of his cruiser, leaving it at a hasty angle in Mary's front lawn. The deputy, formerly patrolling the neighborhood, now spoke with a growing crowd of neighbors along the roadside. EMTs rolled a woman through the grass on a gurney.

Somewhere in the distance, thunder cracked.

West bypassed everyone, charging into Mary's home in search of Tina. "Tina?" he called, both into the phone and into the air. "Where are you? I'm here." She'd stopped talking minutes ago, but he'd refused to hang up. He wouldn't leave her alone and in pain ever again. Not even for a second.

"Here." Her ragged voice echoed over the line and through the empty farmhouse from above.

He stuffed the phone into his pocket and raced to the second floor.

Gentle sobs rolled from the room at the end of the hall where Tina sat, doubled over, on the floor, hugging a teddy bear to her cheek. "She's gone."

The words ripped at West's gut. The agony on her face and in her voice shredded his heart. He fell into place at her side and curled her against his chest like he'd longed to do since he'd first laid eyes on her again. "Hey." He stroked tear-soaked hair from her cheeks and cradled her head against his collarbone. The cell phone clattered from her grip. West swept it away and pulled her body closer. "An Amber Alert has already been issued. It came across my phone and onboard computer. My deputy is talking to Mary's neighbors now, following protocols. We're on top of this. My guys are the best, and we're going to get Lily back. It's everyone's first priority, and we will bring her home to you."

Tina covered her face with both hands and cried harder.

"Tina." He angled his head, straining for a look at her hidden face. "I know this is awful, and I'm an ass for saying so right now, but I need you to pull it together."

Tina stiffened in his arms. She rocked away from him with betrayal in her eyes. He deserved the heated look. It wasn't like her to let her guard down, and he'd told her to knock it off, but he had good reason.

West returned her stare with what he hoped looked like compassion. He had a job to do, and he needed her help. "Your sitter is out cold. I saw her being taken on a gurney. She's my only witness, and she's useless to me until she regains clarity. The neighbors might've seen something. I don't know yet. What I have here and now is you, and I need you."

Tina's eyebrows relented their angry stance. "Me?"

"Yes. Can you tell me if anything other than Lily is missing? A favorite blanket or doll. A diaper bag. Anything like that. Is there anything that should be here right now but isn't?"

"Everything," she cried. "It's all gone, as if he tried to erase her from existence. He even stripped the bedding from her crib. He took her toys. The spare outfits. Anything Mary kept in reserve for her is gone. All he left was this bear." Her voice cracked, but she handed the animal over.

West turned the plush toy around. The bear's tiny

T-shirt had bright golden letters that formed the word *Thomas*. "Thomas was your husband's name."

She chewed her bottom lip roughly, never taking her eyes off the small brown bear.

West considered the newest disturbing fact. The one who stole her daughter had left the bear named after Lily's father. West was no profiler, but it seemed to him the person responsible for this probably planned to replace Lily's father completely. No need to bring a memory of him along.

"What are you thinking?" she asked in a whisper, pushing herself away from him. "I'm missing something. I can see it in your eyes. And don't you dare hold back. I need all the facts right now, West. Don't treat me like a stranger."

West stretched onto his feet and circled the room's perimeter, deciding how to approach the conversation. If there was a bright side, he had to lead with that. Tina needed hope more than ever. "I think it's good that the abductor took all of Lily's things." He opened and closed an empty drawer. "He needs all that stuff to take care of her. He wants Lily to have all the things she needs and loves."

Tina's face brightened. "He plans to care for her."

"Yeah."

"That would be slightly more comforting if he hadn't shot a man today. There's delusion and then there's downright dangerous." Her face crumbled. "I don't want my baby in the hands of a killer."

West returned to her and pressed steady hands to her

quivering cheeks. "We don't know who took her. We need to get all the facts before we lose focus. Okay?"

"Okay."

Outside, the cry of an ambulance broke through the night.

West dropped his hands. "They're taking Mary to the hospital. Someone will be in touch when she's able to answer questions."

Tina squared her shoulders, regaining herself. "Mary had a weak pulse, but it was there. I don't know what happened. I didn't look for the injury." She cupped shaky fingers over her lips. "I left her on the floor. I kept looking for Lily. Oh, my gosh. I'm a terrible person."

West scoffed, then pulled her against him. "I don't know a better person than you. No one blames you for leaving Mary. Not the EMTs, not Mary. No one. You were worried for your baby. What else could you do?"

"Lily's so tiny," Tina choked out. "She's so fragile. If he drops her. Or shakes her."

"He won't," West interrupted. He held her close and stroked her hair. "We're going to get her back, and we're going to find her in the same perfect condition you last saw her in. I swear it."

West's gut fisted at the promise. He meant it, 100 percent, but he couldn't will it to be true, and if he broke this promise, there was no coming back. He'd lose Tina forever. She'd survived a lot of things, but he didn't see her recovering from the loss of her child. Everything about her said that Lily was her life raft. The reason Tina had kept her head up through it all, and someone had taken that from her. West couldn't allow her pain to go on a moment longer than absolutely necessary. He wouldn't.

His heart blistered with empathy as a new round of Tina's sobs broke against his chest.

What was happening today? In his town? To his... *his what*? The mental shock jarred him speechless. Tina wasn't *his* anything. He tightened his arms around her, hating the truth of the thought.

Chapter Six

Tina leaned against West's side as they descended the farmhouse stairs. Her mind flooded with pictures of her baby crying in a stranger's arms, frightened as he ripped her from her safe haven. The images were accompanied by horrific scenarios in which Mary had probably tried to save her by escaping through the back door, only to be violently incapacitated after Lily was wrenched from her hands.

Unlike when Tina had arrived, every light in the house was now on, blinding her sore eyes and illuminating any nook or cranny where the most microscopic piece of evidence might have landed. A smattering of men and woman worked the crime scene inside and out, some deputies, some unknowns, all scouring the immediate area.

Three men huddled near the porch looked up at them as they passed.

"Does that jacket say FBI?" she asked.

"Yes," West answered.

She struggled for a look at West's face. "Why are

they here?" Not that she didn't appreciate the help, but... "Has something else happened?"

He held her tight against his side until they reached his cruiser, cocked half in the driveway and half on the lawn.

Tina nearly fell over when he released her in the driveway. She hadn't realized how much she'd been relying on his strength, in every way, to keep going.

He turned to face her, hands hovering as if she might tip over. His eyes busily scanned the dismal afternoon crime scene. "Child abductions are often handled by the FBI. My brother Blake is FBI. I'm sure the patrolling deputy reached out to him as soon as he knew Lily was gone."

"Blake?"

"Yeah. He lives in town now with his fiancée, Marissa. Blake's a damn good agent. Looks like he's already rallied a few of his team members from Lexington."

Tina scanned the blue coats for Blake. He was always so much older. More grown-up. Her eyes landed on a near replica of West talking to a woman on Mary's porch. He was a little broader than West, with too much hair, but that was definitely him. Her former surrogate big brother was now a federal agent. "I can't believe he did that. That's wonderful," she whispered.

"We've got a good network. We'll find her, Tina."

Tina envied the pride in his voice. She longed for a day when she could feel proud of her family. With a runaway mom and father in prison, she'd be waiting a very long time.

Blake jogged down the porch steps and cut across Mary's muddy lawn, now lined with nosy neighbors.

"West." He stretched a hand out to his brother. "Tina." He nodded in her direction, eyebrows crouched between sharp blue eyes. It was much the same look Cole had given her outside her office after the shooting.

"Got anything?" West asked.

Blake stared into his brother's face for several long beats, unable or unwilling to answer.

A pile of gruesome thoughts clogged Tina's mind once more, and she curled frozen arms around her middle to keep from falling apart all over again.

West slid immediately out of his sheriff's jacket and pulled it over her shoulders. He snaked a broad arm around her waist and dragged her to his chest. "Do you want to sit in the car? I can turn on the heater."

Tina's heart broke at the gesture. To be cared for was wonderful and amazing, but to be so vulnerable was terrifying and nearly intolerable. She pursed her lips and shook her head. What she needed was a way to get in control of her frantic emotions before she went wholly insane from the severity and endless confliction.

West rubbed the chill from her arms and back with one broad palm. "What?" he prompted Blake, who still hadn't answered his question.

Blake walked away, moving slowly toward the

back of West's cruiser. West followed, pulling Tina along beneath his wing.

Successfully distanced from the other investigators, Blake leaned his backside against the car's bumper and lowered himself into Tina's line of sight. "I called in a favor and got some background information on the two members of your group who were missing during the shooting. Your guy Tucker has a long history of addiction problems and erratic behavior."

Tina chewed her bottom lip. She'd never seen that side of him, but survivors were like that. Either they wore the pain around their necks like an albatross, or they hid it so well no one would ever suspect what they'd been through. "That's not uncommon for someone like Tucker," she said, snapping into business mode. Law and order might be in the Garrett blood, but advocacy ran hot in hers. "PTSD patients often look for a way to escape the pain. Drugs and alcohol make easy and unfortunate outlets for folks trying not to deal with their past. Why are you bringing this up? Do you think he fits the profile for this, or are you suggesting he's on a bender?"

"I'm suggesting he's got a history of instability. Sharing facts. Nothing more. It's still early."

West released Tina to stand on her own again. "What about Carl Morgan? Find anything on him?"

Blake raised his heavy brows. "You like him for this?"

"I don't like him at all."

"He wasn't surprised to hear Steven was shot,"

Tina blurted. "It's been on my mind, niggling in the background, since we spoke with him." She'd wanted West to follow the facts, not her paranoia, but it felt good to finally voice the concern.

"She's right," West agreed. "I thought the same thing. I assumed the lack of response could be a side effect of his mental health issues, but he didn't even pretend to care about the victim."

Tina cast a pleading look at West. "I'm not accusing him of anything. I just wanted to put it out there." Carl didn't normally talk much. Whether that was because he's ashamed of the stutter or just hiding his demons, she couldn't say. Either way, he might not have reacted to Steven's death because he simply didn't make a habit of reacting. "Indifference doesn't mean he's a murderer. Right?" She slid her gaze from West to Blake. She knew the answer. Indifference could mean many things to a troubled heart and mind. Though, the more she thought about it, she wasn't sure which specific problems Carl attended her group to resolve. He'd mentioned abuse during his entrance interview, but he'd been stingy with the details. Still was. In group, Carl preferred to be an encourager while others shared, and he watched Tina closely when she spoke. Given the circumstance, she couldn't help wondering if he might've misconstrued her interest in his well-being as personal interest in him. Romantic interest.

Could Carl Morgan be a stalker? A child abductor? And what about Tucker Bixby? Had she somehow given one of them the wrong idea?

Blake shifted his weight. "So far we know Carl grew up in Pine Hurst. That's about ten miles from here, just outside the Cade County lines. He moved to town about sixteen months ago when his mother went to live in the nursing home downtown."

West yanked his phone from his pocket. "Pine Hurst's a pretty good-sized place. They've got a police department over there. I may not have cause to petition for psychiatric records, but police reports are public. Let me see if they've got him in the system, and if so, why." He stepped away from Blake and Tina.

Tina threaded her arms into the too-long sleeves of West's coat. The material was still warm from his body heat and scented by his cologne and body wash. She zipped the front to cover the chill left in his absence.

The rain had stayed at bay since the morning's storm, but wind continued to beat against the trees and everything in sight. Thick gray clouds hung low in the murky afternoon sky.

Tina lifted her eyes to Blake. "Do you think Carl or Tucker could've done this?" She struggled to put the quiet, guarded men she knew into the context of child abductor, someone obsessed with her and possibly also a murderer. Could either man have created silent fantasies about making her dinner or being the father figure in her little family of two?

She struggled to swallow the acidic burn of bile rising up her throat.

"Maybe." Blake watched her carefully, seeming to

scrutinize her every breath, as if deciding whether or not *she* was a suspect in his investigation.

"What?" she snapped, sounding exactly as impatient as West had minutes before.

His eyes flicked to West, busily speaking with someone from Pine Hurst on his phone, then back to her. "How long have you and my brother been talking again?"

She looked at her watch. "About five hours. He came to the office after the shooting."

"What about before that?"

"You probably heard about the time before that." Her chin inched higher, prepared to defend herself for the inexcusable behavior. She had been wrong not to open up to West about her reasons for leaving back then, but she was also very young and broken. She'd needed more than a boyfriend to heal her pain.

"You bought a home here," Blake said. "When did you move back?"

"About two years ago." She struggled to remember the exact date, but Blake was clearly looking for more. "A few months after Dad went to jail, I guess." Her father should've gone to jail long ago, but he was making up for it with ten to life now. His drunken outbursts had finally hurt him almost as much as his victim.

Blake's eyes jumped again to West. "Yeah?"

"Yeah." Shame and guilt plugged her throat. According to police reports, someone half her dad's age had mouthed off to him at a bar, and her dad couldn't let it go. He lit into the guy, but age and alcohol had slowed him, and for once his victim wasn't afraid. When the young guy got the best of him, her dad had hit him with a broken bottle, then stabbed it into his side. The victim lived, but he pressed charges, and somehow every call the police ever made to her childhood home came crashing down on him, sealing her father's fate with a maximum sentence.

Tina had come home when her mom stopped answering the phone. She'd worried about the frail woman who'd spent most of Tina's life hiding in bed, nursing fresh wounds delivered by the hands of her husband. Sadly, without her father to hold her hostage, her mother had fled. Tina had laid down new roots in Shadow Point, praying for her return.

West pocketed the phone and turned back to Tina and Blake. "Pine Hurst PD is willing to cooperate. They're searching their database for anything they have on Carl. They'll get back with me as soon as they have something."

Blake nodded. "We're looking for the pharmacist. He wasn't home or answering his phone."

West widened his stance and crossed his arms. "All right. Anything else?"

Blake's eyes were locked on Tina. "West said your husband was in a hunting accident?"

Tina's mouth opened, but words failed her. Rehashing the loss of Thomas was more than she could manage, and she felt her mind shutting down.

Blake dragged his pointed gaze to West. "Shooter used a 30-06 today."

Tina slid her eyes closed. A hunting rifle. *Like the*

one that killed Thomas. Her world shifted beneath her. "That was more than a year ago," she said, fear and panic churning in her soul, cracking her voice and composure in one fell swoop. "What you're suggesting is impossible. I'm not stupid. I haven't been stalked for a year."

Blake was watching her when she opened her eyes. He didn't speak.

Tina covered her mouth, muffling a strangled sob. The ache in her throat spread to her eyes and pounded in her head. It couldn't be true. Her husband's death couldn't have been murder. It was an accident. Wasn't it? She clenched her fists to stop the tremor rocking through her hands, and willed her legs to hold her upright as the weight of the revelation did its best to knock her down. "Why is this happening?"

"Garrett?" a distant voice called. Someone in a blue jacket waved one hand overhead.

Blake walked away.

"We don't know," West said. "This is the part where we run down every scenario. Even the ugly ones." He guided her to his passenger door and helped her inside. "Let's get Ducky and head to my place for the night. You can stay there for as long as it takes us to find the person who's doing this. I guarantee you no one will come near you there."

Tina swung her feet inside, and the door shut hard enough to rattle her teeth. He grabbed the bags from the passenger side of her unlocked car and tossed them onto his back seat. She'd never seen West angry before, but he looked fit to kill, and she didn't doubt his promise of safety for a second.

WEST PULLED INTO Tina's drive, ready to collect her puppy and get her to safety. The deputy hadn't had a chance to process and sweep Tina's home. He was still on Mary's lawn talking to federal agents. It was just West and Tina now.

"Listen," he said, "I'm sorry about Blake. If he made you uncomfortable. I can only guess what he was saying while I was on the phone. If he overstepped, you have my apologies. He's not thinking like an old friend right now. He's thinking about nailing the son of a gun who took your baby."

"Blake was fine," she said softly. "He didn't say anything about our past, if that's what you mean." She tugged the cuff of her sleeve, fidgeting with an invisible thread. "I am sorry, though. About the way I ended things."

He angled to face her in the warm front seat. "Then why did you?"

"I loved you," she said. "That was never the problem. I left because my family was a nightmare, and I thought I was destined to be one, too. You deserved better, and I needed out. It seemed like the right thing to do at the time."

West bit back his opinion on the way things should have been. "That was a long time ago," he managed. "I've never held a grudge."

"No. You wouldn't." She deflated against the back

of the seat. "None of this day feels real. It's like the worst dream ever."

"That's the stress," he said. "Your mind's putting distance between you and the horror so you can process it." He stopped short. "Of course, you already know that."

"Yeah, but it's good to hear. Do you really believe Lily's okay? He didn't take her so he could hurt her or…" She exhaled a long, quiet breath.

"He's not going to hurt her." West hovered a hand over hers, but pulled it back. He had to be the sheriff, not some old flame, consumed with her presence or rekindling the past. He had a job to do. And truthfully, getting too close to Tina right now would make losing her again all the worse when he put her life back together and she walked away.

Tina unlocked the door to her home, and West led the way inside.

Tina flipped every light switch she passed until the house was fully lit.

West cleared the rooms. "We're alone," he said, holstering his sidearm. He hadn't expected to find the killer waiting on her again, but it was better to be prepared than surprised.

Ducky whimpered in his cage, waiting impatiently where they'd left him hours before. West crouched to unhinge the latch. "I bet you need to go out."

"Woof!" Ducky wagged his tail and attempted to hop and pounce in the locked crate.

"If you need anything else, now's the time to get it," West advised Tina. "I'll take Ducky out and walk your perimeter before we load up. Keep the doors secured while I'm gone."

"Thank you for doing this," she said.

He caught her weary stare and forced a tight smile. "Anything and always."

He opened the door for Ducky, and chastised himself for using their old words of endearment now. What had possessed him? Hadn't he just told himself to back off five minutes ago? The woman had lost everything, yet there he was trying to get back into her heart. As if he wasn't the reason her dad got a maximum sentence and her mother was in the wind. West shook his head. He hadn't predicted her mother's reaction to her father's sentence. If he had, he never would have pushed. Now it was too late, and once Tina understood the role West had played in her family's disintegration, she'd never speak to him again.

Ducky chased smells on the wind and through the grass with gusto, running full speed, then stopping repeatedly to jam his nose into the rain-soaked lawn.

West flicked his flashlight beam over the shadowed ground. He'd assumed the primary crime scene was inside when they'd arrived the first time. Strange how quickly things could change.

He kicked a boot through the tall grass at the back of Tina's property. The tree line stood thick and foreboding, less than a dozen yards from her home.

From his new vantage point, West had a clear view of Tina's kitchen, living room and bedroom. The windows of her home glowed like a television screen against the night. He watched, mesmerized, as she ghosted past the glass, a silent movie to which any lunatic could add his own script.

West went back to work, only to discover something far worse than the view. His heart thudded dangerously at the discovery of a large matted section of grass. A thermos and cooler were masked by the low-hanging cover of an evergreen branch. The remnants of a sandwich wrapper rustled in the wind, caught on the edge of a hardened shaft of a weed.

West lowered into a crouch and marveled at the view of Tina's home. Someone had scouted the property line and chosen the best spot for his twisted voyeuristic games.

West needed someone out here to collect and process the evidence before another storm came and washed it all away. He snapped photos and forwarded them to his team with the directive to get over there as soon as possible, then he checked the cooler and thermos contents. Water in the latter, packaged jerky and melted ice in the former. The grass was dead beneath the cooler. Whoever came here did so often enough that they'd stopped hauling supplies back and forth. It was the equivalent of having a drawer for your things at your girlfriend's house. If your girl was an unsuspecting single mother you stalked from the property line.

A tight knot wound in West's gut as he watched Ducky roam the yard. Ducky knew his territory. He knew every scent. What belonged. What didn't.

Ducky hadn't attacked the intruder earlier because he knew him.

She'd gotten the dog following the loss of her husband.

The psycho had always been a part of her dog's life. How many times had the killer been inside Tina's home? Played with her dog? Her daughter? Was Tina ever there when he crept through her rooms?

West raised his eyes to the graceful silhouette floating through a golden backdrop of lamplight. His muscles tightened, balling both hands into fists. Tina Ellet had been his first true love, and like it or not, his heart had never fully released its claim on her. Whoever had done these things was going to pay, and when he knew she was safe, West was going to win her back.

Chapter Seven

Headlights drew Tina's attention to the front window. West was in the backyard with Ducky, and she had no intention of opening the door to anyone without him. Whoever had just arrived could walk around the house and meet him out back. Not to be rude, but she simply couldn't face another lawman right now. Her daughter was missing, and Tina was in no mood to play hostess.

She pressed the soft fabric of Lily's favorite blanket against her cheek and fought another round of heart-wrenching sobs. The sweet scent of baby wash pinched her chest and stung her eyes.

Where was her baby?

The headlights continued to shine against her window without blinking out. No slamming car doors. No footfalls upon her porch stairs. Just a gloomy October afternoon and a set of blinding headlights.

Tina hugged the blanket to her chest and pulled the curtain back for a peek. She dropped the little quilt, having been nearly blinded, and blinked her vision back to normal. No one was in her drive. The light was coming from a truck parked on the curb across the quiet intersection from her home.

Fear pressed her back a step.

Was she overreacting, or was some other horrible thing about to happen?

She freed the phone from her pocket, then peeked outside again. What if the shooter was in that truck? Or her stalker? Or her daughter? What if Lily was only a few yards away, and Tina still couldn't reach her? "Pick up," she whispered to the ringing phone.

"Garrett," West answered.

Tina wet her lips and willed her voice to come. "There's someone out front," she whispered. "A truck with its bright lights on, and they're pointed into my living room."

"Stay inside," he snapped.

The call disconnected.

Tina rolled her shoulder against the wall. She lifted her head for one more glance through the window. A familiar shape streaked across the yard and into the flood of light. *No.*

"Ducky!" Tina swung the door open with bumbling hands.

The driver's door opened and a man stepped out, scooping her dog into his arms and dropping him into the pickup's bed before returning to his place behind the wheel.

Panic welled and boomed in her, beating between her ears and pounding in her chest. "Ducky!" She scrambled into the yard. "Come!"

An arm stretched through the open driver's-side window and motioned her closer, but her dog stayed.

With a stranger?

"Stop!" West's voice echoed through the air. He moved into Tina's peripheral vision, weapon drawn. "Cade County Sheriff," he announced, moving steadily toward the truck. "Get out and put your hands up!"

The pickup's engine growled and roared. Powerful amounts of torque tilted the faded red pickup with each press of the gas, successfully drowning West's demands for subordination.

Ducky barked and paced the truck bed, tail wagging.

Tina's stomach rolled. It was the pickup that she'd seen fleeing the shooting this morning. Her dog knew this man? Chose to ride in the truck over returning to her? How often had Ducky seem him? How well did Tina know the truck's driver? Had she invited him to her home? Had he made the trip on his own more often that just this day?

Who would do something like this? What had she done to him that had caused this? Her baby wasn't enough? He'd even come for her dog? She pressed desperate palms to the sides of her head, protecting her ears and attempting to hold her mind together.

West continued his approach, gun up, wrists locked. He stepped slowly and confidently into the blazing light. His mouth moved, but the words were smothered by the revving truck.

Slowly, the doors on neighboring homes began to

open. Folks spilled onto their porches, only to take note of the armed sheriff and dash back inside.

The engine reduced to a steady purr, and West moved into the light. "I won't say it again. Get out now."

The truck's tires barked, and the vehicle lurched forward with a roar.

"West!" Tina screamed as the pickup careened onto the sidewalk, heading straight for the sheriff.

West dove out of the way, colliding with the pavement in a wild roll as the truck fishtailed back onto the street.

"West!" Tina slid to a stop against his side, grinding pebbles from the sidewalk into her knees and shins. The truck had escaped with her dog and another piece of her broken heart. "West!" She fell onto his chest, pressing her cheek to his motionless torso. "No!"

A low groan rumbled against her ear. Heavy arms wrapped around her trembling frame. "I'm okay."

Tina pulled back for a closer look at his filthy, bloody coat and face.

"I'm all right." He shoved into a sitting position, dusting his arms and stretching his neck with a wince. He ran a fist under his bloodied nose and grimaced. "Ow."

Tina brushed dirt from his stubble-covered cheek. "I thought you were dead."

He shot her a disbelieving look. "Please. I'm not that easy to kill."

She pulled him to her again and squeezed. "Thank

goodness because I can't lose you, too," she whispered, utterly horrified by the possibility. Someone as truly good and selfless as West Garrett was not the sort of man a woman should ever let go. She'd already done that once, and she preferred not to let it happen again.

He rubbed her back and cleared his throat. "I'm not going anywhere."

"Good." She hooked her flyaway hair behind one ear and tried not to be sick. "Do you think Lily was in that truck?" Her stomach knotted as she imagined her infant in a vehicle driven so recklessly. One mistake. One small error. She couldn't bear to think of the potential consequences.

West ran a gentle palm along Tina's cheek. "I don't know."

"Woof!"

Tina jumped at the blessed sound. "Ducky!"

The retriever hobbled toward her, tail beating behind him. *"Woof!"*

She released West and pulled the dog onto her lap.

Beside her, West pressed onto his feet and reported the truck situation to Dispatch.

Tina held Ducky tight and promised herself Lily would soon be in her arms again, as well.

WEST FINISHED HIS call while checking his limbs and appendages for range of motion and functionality. Everything seemed to be in working order, though his ribs and nose were a little worse for wear. "I put a bulletin out on the truck," he told Tina. "I missed the plate, but I got a real close look at the vehicle, so I think I nailed the description. It was the one you saw this morning. Wasn't it?" She nodded.

"I figured." He limped several steps, testing his legs and ankles with a hearty grunt. Between that roll on the pavement and the recent knock on the head, West was nearing his daily capacity for physical beat-downs. "Damn. I'm not twenty-five anymore." He rolled his shoulders and shook out his arms. Nothing was broken, but he felt like maybe he'd have been better off getting hit by the truck.

West pulled Tina onto her feet. "Come on. Let's get Ducky's things and get out of here." He needed to go somewhere he could rest and heal.

"Shouldn't we wait for the ambulance? You need to let a medic take a look at you."

"Nah." West urged her toward the front door. "I didn't call an ambulance."

"You were just hit by a truck!" She struggled to slow him down as he nudged her forward. "You need an exam at least."

"I wasn't hit. I've been hurt worse, and most of this mess will come off in the shower. Now, move."

Ducky hopped along at their feet until they reached the steps, but stopped without attempting the climb.

"You, too," West told him. "Let's go." He pulled the retriever into his arms and nodded at Tina and the house. "A little help?"

She rushed inside, bracing the door for them to pass. "I don't understand why no one's coming here? A madman just sat outside my home while we were inside. He tried to steal my dog, nearly killed my…" Her mouth snapped shut. Her chest rose and fell with several short breaths. "You."

West wished like hell she'd have finished that sentence, but that would have to wait. "I've got limited resources, and this nut is everywhere today. Blake's sending a man out to talk to your neighbors. He'll get here as soon as he finishes at Mary's. Meanwhile, if you give your vet a call, I'll see if being the sheriff can get Ducky seen immediately. Then we'll head to my place, where I can clean up and review all the data we gathered today. It'll probably take me until dawn to wade through everything. Maybe you can get some rest."

Tina stared through her front window. "I'll go to your place tonight, but I won't sleep." Not until Lily was home safely. "Maybe I can come up with some characteristics for a profile on the kind of person who'd do this, then form a list of every person I've ever met who fits the bill. Maybe something I think of will help Blake's team find this guy."

West smiled. There was fire in her eyes again. That was the woman who had tossed his teenage world into upheaval, and he was mighty proud to be back at her side. "Atta girl. This guy didn't live in a bubble before today. He has friends, coworkers, relatives, neighbors. One of those people will be willing to assist in his capture and the safe return of your daughter."

West loaded Tina and Ducky into the cruiser.

He gave Tina a long look at the first stoplight. Even with a background in counseling, he couldn't imagine how anyone could deal with all she'd been put through today. "Hey."

Tina turned unseeing eyes on him; exhaustion and grief twisted her pretty face.

"What did you do while you were away all those years?" he asked, hoping to be a distraction from her sorrow.

"College," she answered flatly, a note of disappointment in her tone. "Undergrad. Grad school. Internships. After that, I shared a chic little apartment above a yoga studio with a New York City transplant named Elise. She grew sprouts in a window box and blended them into smoothies with kale and bananas." Tina offered West a small smile. "I know what you're doing."

"What?" He feigned innocence. "I'm curious. Can you blame me? I missed out on a third of your life."

"You're trying to keep me from going into shock or completely over the mental edge. I know. I do it with patients in crisis."

He motored through the green light and took the next turn toward the local veterinarian on Main. "Sounds like you had an interesting time. The only thing I put in my blender is margarita mix."

"We did that, too."

"Did you ever get homesick?"

She leveled him with a pointed look. "The only thing I've ever missed about this place was you."

West pressed his lips tight. The only thing she'd missed was him? What the hell was that supposed to mean? She hadn't missed him enough to come home. Not even for one night. Not in a decade. She hadn't missed him enough to make a phone call and say so or return an email. He'd kept the same account open since high school, hoping that one day she'd reach out to him. He'd checked for that message every day while he was overseas, hoping she'd realize what they had was special. Worth fighting for. "Why'd you come back?" he finally asked. It certainly hadn't been for him. She'd been home two years without ever saying hello.

"My mom," she answered softly, then turned her face toward the windshield, shutting him out all over again.

West gripped the wheel tighter. It was his fault her mom had run. He needed to tell her the truth about that, but now wasn't the time. She needed some good news today, not more things to break her heart. And he'd prefer to remind her why they'd been great together, not give her more reasons to run.

"What'd I say?" she asked. "You're grinding your teeth hard enough to break them."

He jerked his head back. "Nothing."

She huffed and crossed her arms. "You always sucked at lying. You want to keep it to yourself? Go ahead."

He would.

He swung the cruiser into the lot outside the vet clinic and climbed out. He needed to get his head in the game and off his battered heart.

He shut his door a little more roughly than necessary and opened the back for Ducky.

The whole thing was ridiculous, to be thinking about her like that at a time like this. He hefted the dog into his arms and jammed the back door closed with one hip. Maybe *he* should get some therapy when this was over.

A narrow hand poked into view and pulled the clinic door open for him. Tina stood back so he and Ducky could enter the building. "You didn't think I was going to wait in the car, did you? With a lunatic stalking me?" She marched to the desk and smacked one palm against the little silver bell on the counter.

West lowered Ducky onto the floor and found a seat. He positioned himself for the best view of the clinic's window, door and empty lot.

A man in a white lab coat spoke softly to Tina before handing her a clipboard and pen.

A moment later, she lowered herself into the chair at West's side. "I'm really angry." She scribbled her contact information onto the paper, a look of frustration on her brow. "I want to just go crazy, blow up and fight, but there's no one to fight. None of this makes sense. It's not real."

"You can fight with me, if it helps." He tapped the toe of his boot against her sneaker.

Her cheek kicked up. "I don't want to fight with you."

"You sure?" He shifted in his seat and grimaced. His ribs were more sore than he'd thought, and sitting still was only making it worse. "I'm tougher than I look."

"You look like crap." She rolled her eyes and deposited the clipboard on the floor with Ducky. "Let me see your ribs." She reached for the hem of his shirt.

"Hey, now." He pressed the fabric back over his tender flesh.

Tina scoffed. "Baby. Move your hands."

"Excuse me?" He frowned. "I was hit by a truck."

"If that truck had connected with you, you never would've gotten up." She pushed his hands away and dragged the shirt up for a better view of his torso.

West stopped fighting when she made a little sound. The expression on her face was perfection. "See something you like, doc?"

She blinked, then dropped the shirt as if it had burned her. "Just bruising. A hot shower, aspirin and ice will help."

"Are you sure?"

She nodded and gathered the clipboard back into her hands.

"You can look again if you want."

She shook her head and went back to writing on her paper. "Shut up." Her cheeks darkened under his stare, reminding him of other times he'd coaxed a rush of color into her skin. She slid her eyes his way, then put them back on the task before her.

There was something she wanted to say, but she was fighting it. He could see it in her eyes when she'd moved her gaze in his direction. The look was there when he'd returned her to her car earlier, and it was there again now.

He hoped she'd change her mind this time. He

couldn't take being shut out again, and he didn't want to let her go. West returned his attention to the world beyond the clinic window, but damn it if his heart wasn't seated in the chair right beside him.

Chapter Eight

Tina watched with rapt curiosity as the cruiser wound along desolate country roads. She'd never given much thought to where West hung his hat, but now that they were on their way to his place, she couldn't stop thinking about it. Clearly, he hadn't chosen a traditional neighborhood. Those were all behind them now, tucked closely together near the center of town. She imagined if he had his choice, he'd live on a small farm or in a cabin. West was an outdoorsman through and through. It was his love of nature that had drawn her to him, and his love for people that held her there to the very end. Amazing how she appreciated those qualities all the more as a grown woman.

The cruiser slowed near a bend in the road, and West turned onto a narrow drive nestled between ancient oaks and evergreens. The forest rose into the sky on either side, tangling their limbs in leafy patches overhead. "Here it is."

"Talk about secluded," Tina marveled. "Don't you get lonely?"

He smiled through the windshield. "Not with all this."

They rocked down the gently pitted drive in silence, listening to songbirds and crunching gravel before a handsome log cabin came into view. A wide expanse of lawn extended in every direction, seemingly cut from the hills just for him. No, West wouldn't be lonely here, surrounded by nature and just minutes from all the friends and family a person could want.

West gathered her bags and swung Tina's door open. "You're smiling."

"This is beautiful."

"Thanks. I bought the land when I came home from the service. Dad, Cole and I restored the house. It was pretty well run-down, dilapidated, collapsed roof, but it was part of Shadow Point's story, so we gutted it and started over inside. It needed just about everything replaced, but the bones were solid, and I like living in a piece of our town's history." He led the way toward his home, saddled with her things. "This used to be the office of an old mining company. I found some pictures at the library and framed them for the mantel. The house is small, but it's been plenty big enough for me."

The sun had set while they'd waited for Ducky to be seen and treated. A while longer still for paperwork when she'd decided he was safer being boarded with her trusted veterinarian than going home with her and West.

Tina followed him along a flagstone path to the

porch, admiring his landscaping and the tire swing suspended from a massive oak in the front yard. It was like having a deeper look inside the man West had become. "That swing is just like the one at your folks' house."

"Yeah. Didn't seem like home without one, though I'm not sure anyone's ever used it. I don't get much company and Cole stopped swinging years ago." He flashed her a mischievous smile.

"Good to know." She gave the tree another long look before moving on. She hoped that one day Lily would swing on a tire like that, happy and carefree, oblivious that childhoods like Tina's existed.

West shoved the cabin door open and flipped on the lights. A cozy living space sprung into existence before her eyes. "Wow."

"Thanks." West locked the door. "We put the loft and stairs in. It'll be my office once I get the electrician out here to wire it, but it could also be a guest room with a little work. I'm going to put your things in my bedroom. I'll take the couch, and you can do whatever you'd like. I don't plan on sleeping, but you should try."

Tina followed him down a wide hall to a pair of doors facing off with one another.

He pointed to the left. "That's the bathroom, and this—" he turned to the right "—is the bedroom." He hit the light switch, then delivered her bags to the bed.

Tina wandered inside, admiring the comfortable-looking bed and trying hard not to let her mind wander to where Lily was sleeping tonight. Allowing her thoughts to wander was the worst sort of torture, and she needed to hold it together a little while longer.

She had solid plans to cry herself to sleep at the first opportunity. "This is beautiful."

"I made it from trees on the property. We had to take them down to make room for my pole barn." Thick, polished limbs and logs were twined together to form the headboard and bedposts. The mattress was nearly waist high and covered with a pale gray duvet.

West watched her curiously as she took it all in.

She'd felt the way he looked not long ago, when West had gone through her home, room by room. She'd been irrationally anxious, wondering what he thought of her life, and if he knew how important it was to her that he approved. She couldn't be sure about the second part, but West was undoubtedly feeling as exposed as she had while he'd plucked through her personal space.

She circled the room, taking in the details. Everything smelled like aftershave, leather and spice. A row of belts hung from the open closet door, and a line of boots stood against it. Stacks of blue jeans and T-shirts climbed the closet interior, supported by a framework of wooden shelves. He'd probably made those, too.

A photo of several men in fatigues sat on his dresser. Most of the group members were shirtless. All were tattooed. West included. Dark lines of india ink wrapped their arms, chests and sides. She turned curious eyes on him.

"Army buddies," he said.

"You got a tattoo?"

"Couple." West cleared his throat and leaned against the doorjamb. "It was nice of the vet to keep Ducky, but I didn't mind bringing him here."

A change of subject? West didn't want to talk about the tattoos. Why? She bit her lip against the nosy question, and went with his new subject instead. "Dr. Flanders's wife is a friend of mine. I know he'll take good care of Ducky while I'm away, and I have no idea what comes next for me, so I think he's better off there than here. I'm just glad he only needed a bandage." Ducky was lucky that leap from a moving vehicle hadn't done worse than some muscle strain. "Speaking of injuries." She walked back to West. "You need to clean your scrapes and cuts, and put a butterfly bandage on your chin or you could wind up with a scar. You'll also want to put some ice on your worst bruises, or they'll hurt like hell in the morning."

West shook his head, clearly amused by her list of orders. "Yes, ma'am."

His slow Southern drawl sent her back to high school, when those words had been his standard response for personal requests, like a toe-curling kiss or a rendezvous under the bleachers after class. Heat bled across her cheeks.

West grabbed a small stack of clothes from his closet, then turned for the door. "Give me ten minutes to shower, then I'll make coffee and we can get started on the killer's profile. I don't need ice or bandages." He glanced at the bed. "If you'll try to rest, I'll try to hurry."

Tina watched as he dropped his things on the bathroom counter across the hall and stared into the mirror. He unbuttoned his uniform shirt and let it fall onto the floor before grabbing the hem of his white undershirt and stripping it off over his head. Thick, taut muscles worked across his back and chest as he removed the material and tossed it aside, leaving a clear view of his sharp, lean torso. West had always been fit, but now…wow. Expertly detailed tattoos lined his ribs, arm and shoulder. The words were dressed as badges, painted on military choppers and replica dog tags. Words like *Ranger. Airborne.* And *All Gave Some. Some Gave All.*

She pressed a palm to her stomach, no longer lean from youth and hunger, in an attempt to stop the butterflies. Her body had changed as much as West's, though not in the same ways. He was broader and thick from military training and an outdoorsman's life. She was softer, curvier from the effects of maternity and a regularly filled stomach. Sure, her hips were wider and her bottom more round, but she'd never felt as beautiful. She couldn't help wondering if West had noticed the physical changes in her, too. If he had, what did he think?

West turned to look across the hall at her, as if he'd somehow heard her unspoken question. He unbuckled his belt and slid it from the loops. His hands lingered at his waist, and his soulful blue eyes fixed hungrily on her.

Tina's heart hammered and her chin dropped. "Oh, my God. I'm so sorry." She was caught staring. Caught watching the man undress. "I didn't… I wasn't…" She waved her hands helplessly between them. She wasn't what? Imagining what his new body would feel like pressing down on hers? "Oh, Lord." She marched to the open bedroom door and swung it shut before she died of humiliation.

WEST CHUCKLED SOFTLY and rubbed a heavy palm over his cropped hair. He'd been caught in the midst of a fantastically filthy fantasy. Worse, he'd been caught by the woman who was starring in it. If Tina's expression was any indication, the images he'd unintentionally conjured were painted on his face. He'd been enjoying the imagined reflection of her bare backside in the bathroom mirror while she sat on the counter, legs wrapped tightly around his waist.

And *damn*.

He'd looked across the hall to find her staring back. Her face was six shades of red, and he couldn't muster a single explanation. Though, she'd panicked enough for the both of them.

He rushed through his shower and re-dressed in his favorite blue jeans and old army T-shirt, hoping she wouldn't ask what he'd had on his mind when their eyes had met. He wasn't a fan of lying, and she probably wouldn't like the truth. Luckily, the steaming hot water had cleared his mind and helped him refocus.

West wrenched the bathroom door open and padded into the kitchen on bare feet. Scents of black coffee and scrambled eggs rose to meet him.

Tina sat cross-legged on a stool at his island, sipping from an old mug. "Sorry. I realized I was starving, and figured you were, too." She cringed. "I should've asked before I made myself at home in your kitchen."

West ignored the warmth blooming in his chest. The view before him was one he'd always wanted, but it wasn't real. They weren't sharing a meal, coffee and conversation because they wanted to. They were here because she was in danger, and it was up to West to protect her. Nothing more.

He poured some coffee and shoveled eggs onto a plate. "You don't have to ask. You're a guest. What's mine is yours." He opened his laptop on the counter and printed the new findings from Tina's case and the shooting. "I've got enough work here to keep me busy. The shower's free and so's the bed. Help yourself to whatever you need. I'll be here in my temporary office for a while."

Tina set her cup aside and dusted her palms together. "Okay. First, do you mind if I take a look at those bruises?"

West concentrated on his email. "I'm fine." He could probably use some ice or aspirin like she'd suggested earlier, but he definitely didn't need her hands roaming over his skin. He was only human.

She slid off the stool and approached him behind the counter, where his printer expelled page after page of documentation.

He gathered the papers from the printer and tapped them against the counter, creating a tight stack. "Look at all this." He dragged his phone from his pocket and swiped the screen to life. "Three new texts and a voicemail. How long was I in the shower?" Couldn't have been more than a few minutes. He'd made sure of it. West scrolled through the texts, hoping for some good news, then dialed into his voicemail and put it on speaker.

"West." Cole's voice rang into the air. "We got our hands on the other patient. Tucker. He was on a bender, out camping in the national park. I'm hauling him in for questioning, but he's a mess. By the look and smell of him, he hasn't been in any condition to shoot or drive for a couple days. No word on the truck or baby yet, and no indication an infant or anyone else was with Tucker out here. I'll keep you posted." The message ended and West pocketed the phone.

Tina frowned. "So, it wasn't Tucker. That's good, but I wish he wasn't using again. I wish I could talk to him. Find out what's going on."

"You've got enough to worry about. Let Tucker worry about himself right now." West rubbed his cheek, lost in thought. "Hopefully Chris the pharmacist turns up with an alibi tomorrow. Blake tried to reach him at home and work, but Chris wasn't at either place."

Tina studied the floor. "I didn't consider Chris a serious person of interest until someone took Lily. Now I keep thinking how adamant he was that I join him for dinner or coffee while I was pregnant.

He's left me alone since then, more or less, but that's strange, right?"

"Maybe." West couldn't help but understand any man's desire to know Tina better, pregnant or not. What he thought was strange was the encounter he'd had with her other patient, Carl. That guy might not have been a killer, but he was weird, and something told West that Tina should stay away from him. Though, he doubted she'd take that advice since she was on a quest to save the world.

The heel of his hand caught on his aching chin and he sucked air.

"West." Tina crammed into his personal space, pressing herself between him and the row of cabinets at her back. "Let me see that cut." One small hand landed on the stubble of his cheek. Her thumb fanned over the swollen section of his jaw and lingered near the cut on his chin. "It's bleeding again. You need a bandage. Do you have one?"

He wiped a napkin against his chin, capturing a tiny drop of blood. "This ain't bleeding. This is nothing."

"It isn't nothing," she argued. Her gaze slid from his chin to his lips and lingered. "You need to treat that cut."

"Yes, ma'am." The words were out before he'd intended. He'd used the old line on her earlier to see if it ruffled her feathers, but this time the context was right and so was the mood. The words had come on instinct.

Tina's face drifted closer to his and her free hand

curled against his collarbone. The world stilled as the fragrance of her engulfed him. Scents of vanilla drew him nearer, and he pulled his head down to hers. Tina's eyelids dipped closed and her breath washed over his lips. He clamped greedy hands over the curves of her full, sexy hips and groaned at the warmth of her breasts pressed firmly against him.

"Tina," he started, his voice sounding far too husky. He rested his cheek against hers and shored up his restraint. "You've had one hell of a day. I don't want to play a part in making it any worse once you're thinking clearly."

"Hey," she whispered, tipping her mouth to his. "Shut up and kiss me."

How could West resist an order like that?

Chapter Nine

West pressed his mouth to hers, savoring the moment. He ached to deepen the kiss, but refused to complicate their already complicated reunion any further. He ran his palms down the length of her arms and twined their fingers together on both hands before breaking the chaste kiss.

Uncertainty pinked Tina's cheeks as she opened her eyes. "Oh." She tried to step away, but West held her fast. "It's okay if you don't want me that way anymore," she said. Her voice was strong and even.

He liked that a lot, but she couldn't have been more wrong. "Tell you what." West formed his most challenging smile and released her hands in favor of skimming his palms over the deep curves of her waist and gripping her sexy hips once more. He pulled them tightly against him and held her there.

Tina gasped. Her lids fluttered and the sound from her lips was nearly enough to undo him.

"I'm going to be a perfect gentleman until this is over," West vowed, "but if you're still interested after that, I'll make sure you know exactly how I want you."

She caught the thick of her bottom lip between her teeth and smiled. "Deal."

"Deal."

TINA SETTLED ONTO the couch and pulled her feet up with her. She balanced a notepad on her lap and tapped a pen to the paper. She needed to distance herself from West and refocus on finding the man who'd stolen her baby and demolished her life. West moved past her toward the fireplace, and the sting of rejection pinched her cheeks. He was right, of course, to put her off. She was in no condition to make decisions, and in her experience sex had always complicated things. She'd trusted very few men with that kind of access to her, and had been unequivocally disappointed in the long run, if not sooner. She put that blame on herself. Physical intimacy still meant too much to her, even in the age of cell phone apps made for hooking up with strangers. Sex required a lot of trust, and trust mattered. Which was exactly why she'd behaved so impulsively. At one time, West had been her rock and her comforter. She'd taken all her broken hearts to him, and he'd made her forget her tears. West Garrett was her protector, and no matter how much time had been lost between them, a part of her had hoped he would work his magic again. Make her believe that everything was going to be okay, and that he'd protect her from anything or anyone who dared say otherwise. If West had accepted her advances, she would've been comforted for a while but devastated to lose him when this was over.

Then again, maybe he knew that. Maybe that was his reasoning.

West pushed logs around inside the fireplace, sending embers into the flue. "I keep asking myself what kind of nut would do all these awful things, and I've got nothing." He swiveled to face her, replacing the poker in an iron rack before taking a seat beside the hearth. "I mean, I know crazy is crazy, and the reason probably makes perfect sense to him, but I don't get it."

Tina wasn't a fan of words like *crazy* or *nut* when referring to mental health, but the anger inside her had found a few much worse things to call the man attacking her from every angle. "I'm not sure," she admitted. "I didn't study profiling, and most of my education and experience centers on trauma survivors. If you're looking for speculation, however, I'd say this person is trying to merge our lives. He's attacked my job. Inserted himself into my home." She paused to force images of a cooler in the tall grass behind her home out of her mind. West had shared his awful findings with her while they waited for Ducky to be seen by the vet. Unthinkable as those photos had been, this lunatic, whoever he was, had done much worse. "And he's taken my baby—" she cleared her thickening throat and pushed ahead "—and come for my dog." She cupped a hand over her mouth, certain she'd be sick. It had been a mistake to try to eat at a time like this, even something as mundane as scrambled eggs.

"Then why you?" West asked. He bent his knees and draped steel arms over them. "Is it because you're you, or because you're a widow? A single mom? A counselor?"

"I don't know."

The muscle in his jaw popped and clenched. "Do you think this guy followed you here from your old town, or is a citizen of my county doing this?"

Tina wrinkled her brow. "You take personal responsibility for thousands of people? That's a heavy burden."

"Kind of comes with the job." A small smile formed on West's lips. "I guess I feel as protective of them as you do of your patients, which is why I'm going to ask this carefully. Could this be the work of one of your group members? Past or present?"

Tina's knee-jerk response was "No, of course not," but she hadn't stopped considering the possibility since the shooting, and the more pointed crimes she'd witnessed today, the more she'd wondered if this was someone she knew. Even Ducky seemed to know the man somehow. Was he someone she'd talked to about her life? Had she unwittingly presented a killer with casual details about Lily and the sitter, her house, dog and job? No. She was guarded by nature, and she hadn't had many people over since Thomas died. Even fewer since Lily had been born. "I've considered it, yes. Abuse survivors could swing wide, exchange feelings of intense grief for action. Form a working plan to re-create a life lost." She released a slow breath for stability. If that theory was true, then she had to face an even more heinous one. "If ballistics can match the shooter's bullet to the one that killed Thomas, then this behavior goes back a year. It's had time to percolate and grow in the killer's unstable mind."

"Walk me through the timeline following your return to Shadow Point."

Tina stroked the soft fabric of her jeans, drying sweat-slicked palms on her knees. "It started when Dad went to jail."

"About two years ago," West said.

"Right." The solemn look in his eye puzzled her. Maybe his father had told him her secrets after all. She flinched at the possible betrayal to her younger self.

"What then?" West pressed.

"Well." She searched for the right details. "I started calling home again. I knew he couldn't beat her to the phone anymore. I'd finally be able to talk to Mom. Except, she rarely picked up. I thought she'd flourish in his absence, but instead she crawled deeper into herself. It was only then that I came to realize that her depression and detachment had nothing to do with me and everything to do with him. His incarceration hadn't set her free—it had set her afloat without an anchor."

West shifted on the floor, resuming his fuss with the growing fire. "So, he wasn't the tyrant and warden I thought he was?"

"No," Tina scoffed. "He was worse." She closed her eyes against the violent memories racing to her mind's surface. "I think that without him, she was too humiliated to face her life. She'd hidden behind his abuse for so long. Letting him control everything. Including her. Mom and I tried to keep it quiet, but I can see now that everyone knew. Maybe not the specifics, but enough, and she'd built her sad life around the abuse and codependency. When that was taken from her, she bailed."

West's jaw set.

Did he know more than he said about her past? How could she ask without giving it all away?

Tina dragged a pen across her paper. "Dad was arrested, and I put my house on the market when Mom stopped taking calls. I came to visit, and the house was empty. Mail was piled in the box. I had to stay and try to find her." She tipped her head back in exasperation. "Not *find her*, find her. I didn't plan on going on an expedition or anything. I assumed if I kept watch, she'd eventually come home, probably in terrible shape, and I'd be here to help her get back on her feet."

West's face turned stricken. "I looked for her."

"What? When?"

"She wasn't gone more than two days before a neighbor reported it. Mail in the box confirmed the timeline. I thought she'd gone on a vacation. Needed time to think. I checked every day after that. Made calls. Contacted extended family and known acquaintances."

Tina bristled. "You didn't call me."

"How?" He gasped, half laughing at the absurdity, half angry that she didn't think he'd tried. "It's not like she had you listed as an emergency contact. She didn't even have an address book in that house. No computer. Nothing. The letters I sent to your last known address came back unforwarded. Your dad wasn't talking when I went to him. You'd vanished."

Tina tipped her chin higher. She'd made a point of starting a new life because the pain from her old one was more than she could bear, and probably the reason she'd chosen her profession. She couldn't save herself or her family, but she could help someone else if they'd let her.

"When you came back, I assigned a new deputy to look after the case and advise if she turned up. I figured you wouldn't be in a hurry to see me or talk about it, and if you were, I'm not too hard to find."

Tina ignored the jibe. Yes, she could've run to West for help, but according to the deputy, her mom was all but a cold case. So, Tina paid her mom's property taxes and hoped for the best. "Then you know I got here, found a job, bought a house and met Thomas a few weeks later."

"I'd heard that, yes," West admitted. "I tried not to keep up with the details, but I heard anyway. Price of living in a small town, I suppose."

She imagined a thread of hurt in West's voice. "We were married on a whim, the most impulsive thing I've ever done. Stupidest, too. Not that I wouldn't do it again," she corrected. "I got Lily out of the deal, but he was never the one. You know?" She flicked a sheepish gaze at him. "Not the one I'd dreamed of marrying."

West's Adam's apple bobbed long and slow, but he didn't speak.

"I had my suspicions about the pregnancy," she babbled on, wishing she'd kept that last comment to herself, "but I wanted to wait to tell him after I confirmed with the doctor. Then he went on his annual hunting trip. Something he said he did with his dad and brothers growing up in Missouri. He went last year in solidarity, even if he couldn't be with them in person. Driven by nostalgia, I suppose. I don't think he'd actually killed anything in years."

Tina wiped a renegade tear from her cheek. It was awful that he'd died alone in the woods, trying to hold on to a special time from his past when she was waiting at home with news about the future. "His family was torn up at the funeral. Bitter and angry. They blamed one another for not coming back here to hunt with him. It was absurd. As if anyone could've stopped his death." She shook her head. "His dad sent flowers to the hospital when Lily was born, but that was it." She'd stupidly thought that Thomas's family would become her family, even in his absence. They hadn't, and that made two families who didn't want her.

West moved to the couch and tugged her against his side. "You and your daughter deserve more than some crappy flowers and angry, uninvolved in-laws. You know that, right?"

"I know that Lily deserves the world."

"And you do, too." He pressed a kiss against the side of her head that felt a lot like a promise, though she didn't dare dwell on what that promise might be.

She forced her thoughts past the moment and back to the subject at hand. "If this is the work of someone from my therapy sessions, past or present, then you should know I run an open and rolling group. That means anyone can request to join during certain months. When I get a request or referral, I like to do a quick evaluation of the candidate to see if they will benefit from what we do and if they will fit the existing dynamic. I look at the source of their trauma, their current situation and personality. It's important that the group can work together. So, for example, a rape recovery group would be exclusively divided by gender, but abuse survivors can be mixed, especially in situations of parental abuse. Same for former military or law enforcement."

West pulled his arm away and angled to look at her face. "What happens in the sessions? How much do you reveal about yourself?"

"My sessions are process based. Members lead the sessions. They share and give feedback among themselves. I'm more of a moderator."

"Anyone ever express any desires to do something like this? Maybe comment on how much they'd like a family like yours?"

"Never."

He turned his attention to her notepad. "So, what's on your list?"

She flipped the page over to reveal a line of names.

"These are all the men I've met and the places I've been since returning to town."

West quirked a brow. "That's a huge list."

"I've been here awhile."

"Cashier at coffee shop? Postman?"

She smiled. "I don't know the whole town by name."

"Park. Gas station. Church."

"I'm trying to be thorough." Tina pulled in a jagged breath. "West?" The thing that had been tearing her apart inside finally forced its way onto her tongue. He would tell her the truth, even if it wasn't what she'd hoped to hear. "Why do you think I never knew anything was wrong before today? How could I have no idea someone was fixated on Lily and me like this? I didn't know we were being watched. Followed. How could I not realize my baby was in danger? Shouldn't that be my instinct?" She pressed a palm over her heart. "Am I a bad mother?"

West's expression crumbled. "No. It means you're sane and human. It means you trust people, you expect good things, and you were busy enjoying your life while a predator was watching." He cocked a knee on the couch between them and leveled her with a flat, no-nonsense gaze. "You said yourself that these people can be chameleons. What kind of mother would you be if you spent all your time looking for them, expecting the worst? That's no way to live, and you had no reason to do that. So, let's stick to the positives here."

Tina nodded.

West lifted a finger and ticked it off with his opposite hand. "We know criminals who do the kinds of things we saw today, like stalking their victims and setting up a deluded romantic dinner, and they probably do those things because they imagine a relationship with the victim. That's a good thing for right now. It means he's unlikely to do anything he thinks might ruin it. He's going to take good care of Lily to show you that he can. The next time he makes contact, he's going to want you, and I think that will be soon. He came for Lily and Ducky in the span of a few hours. Another good thing because if he tries to get near you, he's mine."

Tina blinked. A dangerous thought was solidifying in her mind. Being abducted would mean getting her hands on Lily. If she could somehow slip into the abductor's grasp and fulfill his fantasy, then she could get Lily and find a way to escape. Another sign she was on the edge of losing her mind. She didn't think reckless things like that anymore. Especially when the recklessness would involve Lily.

West would hate that idea. It was dangerous. And crazy. She'd have to keep it to herself for now.

"May I?" West pulled the notepad onto his lap and reached for the pen. "I know some of these people. I can strike a few off. What kind of guy wouldn't do this?"

"Anyone with a stable home life. Someone with a consistent and predictable work history or strong ties to the community." She heaved a sigh. "There isn't a specific profile. We all process differently, and some people just blend in."

West began to draw lines through the names.

"What are you doing?"

"I grew up with some of these guys. A few are friends of Dad's. Others are regular volunteers at the church or live in a neighborhood I'm familiar with. Little League coaches. Married to their jobs. Wives. Mortgages. Two-point-two kids."

She nodded. Someone juggling the typical American dream was an unlikely candidate for this sort of crime spree, but she was slow to discount anyone. Tina knew firsthand how much people could hide.

West returned the notepad to her and headed to the kitchen. He carried his laptop and a stack of files from the printer back to the couch. "Let's see what we have here. Maybe we can narrow your list down a little further."

He worked diligently for a long while, reading and marking papers. Tucking some between himself and the arm of the couch, tossing others onto the coffee table. He checked his phone regularly, as if it might've buzzed, but he'd missed it. He seemed as equally unhappy when there were messages as when there weren't.

Slowly, Tina's interest in West's progress dimmed. Her stinging eyes grew blurry from fatigue, and her lids drooped in exhaustion. When she reopened them, the pile of papers on the coffee table in front of West had quadrupled.

He dug the heels of his hands against his eyes.

"Are you okay?" she asked.

"Yep. I've gone through every page, account and report. Now I'm just waiting for more, and contrasting what we know versus what we need to know. Wondering how to get the latter." He dropped his hands away from his face and moved the laptop to the coffee table, sending an avalanche of papers onto the floor. "I'll send your completed lists to Blake."

He carried her notepad to the kitchen. A moment later, his printer buzzed to life, scanning and saving the pages. West returned with a thumb drive and a determined look. "Time for bed."

"What?"

"Come on, get up. You can't get any rest on a couch." He extended his hand to her.

"No," she protested. "I should stay up with you. What if something else happens?"

West pulled her onto her feet. "You need your sleep. I've got this." He tucked her against his side and squeezed. "We're going to get Lily back in your arms, then she can steal your sleep. How does that sound?"

Her throat clogged with emotion. "Perfect."

"I promise to wake you if anything significant comes up." He led her to his room and turned down the covers. "Now rest. Tomorrow is a new day."

Tina slid between the sheets, immediately and immeasurably thankful for West's stubborn streak. His bed was perfect—warm and inviting. Her muscles unwound on contact.

"Sweet dreams." He pulled the blanket up to her chin and cut the lights on his way out.

Alone for the first time since losing Lily, Tina's heavy heart ached anew as she closed her eyes to the silence of a home without her baby.

Chapter Ten

West jolted awake. He blinked heavy lids at the orange spray of sunlight filtering through the window. Was it dawn? When had he fallen asleep? His phone buzzed on the coffee table beside his laptop and a mountain of useless reports. He lurched for the vibrating cell phone and snatched it up in one hand. "Garrett," he croaked.

"West?" Cole's voice blew through the line. "I'm at the hospital. Tina's sitter just woke up."

Electricity raced over West's skin as he processed the words and their potential meaning. Mary could potentially provide a description of the man who took Lily. "We're on our way."

He cleared his scratchy throat and called for Tina. A moment later, he was at his bedroom door. "Knock, knock." He rapped his knuckles on the wall before stepping into the room.

Tina was upright in bed, eyes wide. "What happened?"

"Mary's awake. We've got to go." He left Tina to get ready, then headed for the living room. He grabbed a fresh uniform from the closet and ducked into the bathroom to change. A moment later, he pocketed his keys, stuffed his wide-brimmed hat over unkempt hair and winced at the tender lump on the back of his head. West would *really* like to return the favor when he found out who'd jumped him inside Tina's mudroom. He threaded his arms into the soft sleeves of his Cade County Sheriff's jacket and turned back for Tina.

She flew down the hallway, passing him on her way to the front porch, still rubbing sleep from her eyes. "What did Mary say?"

"I don't know. Cole only said she's awake. I want to talk to her before the doctors take her for testing, wear her out or drug her up and leave her too exhausted to answer my questions."

Tina hopped along beside him through the brisk dewy morning, tugging the backs of untied shoes over her heels. "The medical team wouldn't do that," she protested. "They have to know we need her before they take her away. My daughter's life is at stake."

West stopped to unlock the doors to the cruiser. "They don't do it to get in the way. They've got a job to do. We've got a job to do. Problem is, they don't care if we solve our case today or six months from now. Assessing Mary's full medical status is their priority. Getting answers from her is mine. Get in."

West gunned the car's engine to life. He stuck to the speed limits as he headed back into town. The sun scorched a path through the sky before them, blinding and reminding him anything could happen. It was a new day. The shocking emotional charge of yesterday's crime spree had worn into a flat collection of facts. West's mind was clear and focused, thanks to a few unintended hours of sleep, and today was the day West would reunite Tina with her baby. Mary's description of the intruder might even be what makes that possible.

Cole met them in the hospital atrium with an unshaven face and tray of disposable coffees. His uniform shirt was partially unbuttoned and tucked crookedly into his waistband.

Tina greedily accepted the coffee. "Thank you." She wound her fingers around the cup and looked at Cole. "How is she?"

"She's going to be fine." He led the way to the elevator and abused the button with his thumb. "No one's been in to see her yet. Just a nurse making rounds to check vitals." He shifted from foot to foot as he watched the floor numbers illuminate and darken.

West frowned. "Have you slept?"

The doors swept open and Cole dove inside. "A little. Yeah. Come on."

"Have you been home?" Tina asked, parental concern bleeding through her tired voice.

West smiled. He liked this look on her, and it was always fun to aggravate Cole a little.

Cole stiffened. He hated being fussed over. As the youngest of four Garrett brothers, he'd spent more time than he should have trying to prove he wasn't a baby. "I stayed here in case whoever did this decided to keep Mary quiet." He hit the button for the fourth floor and leaned his back against the wall.

"Good work," West said. "How'd it go? Anyone come by who seemed out of place?"

"No, but I caught up with the pharmacist, Chris, this morning. He was at his girlfriend's house last night. Turns out he didn't stop asking Tina out because the baby was born. He stopped asking her out when he started dating this woman."

The doors rattled open, releasing them onto Mary's floor. They followed Cole along a silent hallway, bypassing the nurses' desk with quick nods and a flash of Cole's badge.

He knocked on Mary's door before walking inside. The room was dark despite the morning sun.

"Cole?" Mary's voice was soft and groggy.

"I'm here," he answered, flipping on a dim row of lights along the edge of the room.

She rolled her bandaged head against the pillow and squinted. "Tina." A tear rolled over her ruddy cheeks. "I'm so sorry. I tried to run."

"She's got a concussion," Cole explained. "Light hurts her eyes. Sounds hurt her ears. Movements hurt her head. When she's not sleeping, she's puking."

Tina sat on the edge of Mary's bed and lowered herself to hug the woman. "It's okay. I know you did everything you could, and I'm so sorry you were hurt." She released her with a sniffle. "We're going to find him and get Lily back. These guys will make sure he pays for all these horrible things. I promise. Can you tell us who took her? Or describe him so they can contact the media and get his image out there publicly?"

"No." A sob broke on Mary's lips. "I was watching for you to arrive, and a truck pulled into the drive. It had its bright lights on. I could barely make out the shape of it. I knew something was wrong, so I didn't answer the door. I went to get Lily and wait for the deputy to come back. He was making rounds through the area. I planned to tell him about the truck when he returned, but I heard the front door open." Her chest bounced with shuddered breaths. "I hid in my bed-room closet with Lily. When I thought I heard him leave, I made a run for the back door, but he grabbed me by my hair." Her hand moved higher, stopping at the crown of her salt-and-pepper hair, as if she still felt his fingers there.

West approached the bed, hat in hand, hoping to convey respectful urgency. "Is there anything you can recall about the man who grabbed you? Even the smallest detail can make the difference."

Mary bit into the thick of her bottom lip and shook her head in one tiny move. Her tear-filled eyes locked onto Tina's gaze and the drops rolled freely onto their joined hands.

"It's okay," Tina said. "You might remember some-thing else. Something that's significant, but you don't even realize. How did he smell? Like cigarette smoke, or a familiar cologne? Maybe a topical medicine or a certain food? Anything?"

Mary's lips quivered. "No."

Tina released Mary's hands and gathered her unbrushed hair into a fisted ponytail. "When he grabbed your head, you were holding Lily. Were you holding her when he took her? Did you get a look at his hands or shoes? Were there tattoos on his arms? Was there anything significant about his clothes?"

Mary's head continued to swing infinitesimally from left and right. "No. I'm so sorry." She gasped. "I can't believe I let him take her. I didn't save her."

Tina slid off her bed and turned to pace the room, hands knotted at her middle.

Cole redirected her to an empty but rumpled bed in Mary's semiprivate room. "Mary's going to be fine, and so is your little girl," he promised.

From the looks of it, Cole had made himself comfortable in the spare bed last night. The guy was nothing if not dedicated, and West was damn lucky he'd chosen to become his deputy. Cole could've done anything he wanted with his life, but he'd chosen the same frustrating, heartbreaking, dangerous work as the rest of them. The nut.

Mary sobbed, drawing West's attention back to her.

He dragged a chair to her bedside and lowered himself into it. "Can you walk me through what happened when you reached the back door? Step-by-step."

Mary's eyes darted regretfully to Tina's. "I had one hand on the knob when I heard him behind me. He said, 'Don't make me shoot you,' and I knew he'd do it. I figured he was the one who shot Tina's patient, and maybe he'd meant to shoot her but missed. Maybe he'd gone to my place to wait for a second crack at her. I panicked. I begged him not to shoot. I told him I was carrying a baby." Her words broke into sobs. "If he shot me, then he'd hit her."

West leaned his elbows against his knees, bringing himself closer to Mary's weeping face. "How did he take Lily from you without you seeing him?" Surely he hadn't knocked her out while the baby was in her arms.

Mary plucked tissues from the box at her bedside. "He told me to kneel and close my eyes. I thought he'd kill me, but he told me to lay her on the floor, and that's the last thing I remember."

"Okay," West said. "So, he knocked you out, then took Lily from the floor." He had every opportunity to kill Mary, but didn't. Why? The killer hadn't hesitated to shoot Tina's newest patient, and possibly her late husband, but he'd spared the sitter. Was Mary part of the larger plan to re-create Tina's life somewhere else against her will?

West groaned inwardly. Mary was probably lucky she wasn't abducted to care for Lily, but then again, that would've been a better scenario for Tina and the baby.

Mary pressed wadded tissues to her eyes and choked on a new round of sobs.

"Tell me about the man's voice," West pressed. "Was it especially deep or high? Soft or harsh? Did he have an accent? A drawl? Anything significant to the cadence of his speech?"

Mary cried harder, and West's patience thinned.

Yes, Mary had been through a horrific ordeal, but so had Steven, the dead guy; Tina, the grieving mother; and poor Lily, an infant in the hands of a maniac. "Mary," he pressed.

"West," Cole warned. "Give her a minute."

West's fingers curled tightly over his knees. His jaw locked, and his muscles tensed. How could the only witness to the kidnapping have witnessed nothing?

The second hand on the wall clock ticked loudly overhead, punctuating the passage of time, marking the moments lost in their race to save Lily.

West pinched the bridge of his nose and tried to formulate a new plan for intel. Maybe canvassing Tina's neighborhood would help. Neighbors had come onto the porches at the sound of the truck revving its engine. Maybe someone had seen something else useful recently. A man lurking in the trees or yard, playing with the puppy or entering the house. Maybe they recognized the truck, or had seen it before.

Mary pulled another tissue from the cardboard dispenser. "There was one thing," she whispered.

"What?" Tina's voice sounded from behind him.

The air inside the room thickened with anticipation.

"It's probably nothing," she hedged.

"What?" West prodded.

Mary wrinkled her nose. "He didn't say much. Just those few short sentences, but when he told me to put the baby on the floor…he stuttered."

West's chair scraped against the floor, nearly

knocking into the nightstand in his haste. "Get some-one to Carl Morgan's trailer. Now." He pointed at Cole, who was suddenly on alert. "Get a warrant. Get someone over to see his mama at that nursing home and get his picture all over the damn news!" He strode toward the doorway, still barking orders. He knew that squirrely bastard wasn't right.

Tina gushed her goodbyes to Mary and followed Cole through the door.

Cole contacted Dispatch as they hustled down the hall.

"Tell the first man on location to haul Carl in for questioning and detain him," West said. "We need to get inside that trailer. Talk to the neighbors. He's got that baby."

West's gut clenched. Anger and adrenaline coursed over his skin and pounded in his veins. He'd stood two feet from Carl Morgan yesterday, and he'd walked away. That was before he'd assaulted Mary and kid-napped Lily. "Get his photo added to that Amber Alert along with a description of that pickup truck." West could've prevented this. Now Mary was lying in a hospital bed, injured and sobbing her apologies to Tina for something he'd allowed. It was on him to make this right.

TINA JOGGED DOWN the hallway behind two puffed-up lawmen. The space around them had burst to life since their arrival. Nurses and orderlies marched pur-posefully in every direction, flipping charts and pushing carts. Families poured through the double doors, toting balloons and flowers past the nurses' station.

It seemed unfathomably surreal that none of these people had any idea about what was happening to her. They didn't know that hope had just filled her empty heart until it ached inside her chest.

Cole headed back to Mary's room once the elevator opened.

She and West climbed aboard, waited through a painfully slow descent, then sprinted to the parking lot.

Tina's thumping heart twisted and jumped in her chest. Images of her little girl flooded her mind as she climbed into West's cruiser and buckled up beside the uncharacteristically quiet sheriff. This was the part where he should be thrilled. Proud, even. Saying things like, *Everything is going to be okay.* The nightmare was over. She was safe. Lily was safe. The bad guy was going away for a very long time.

He jammed his foot against the gas pedal and peeled through the parking lot. A drastic contrast to the care he'd taken on their way to the hospital.

Tina watched his face turn slowly redder as he drove. "I've never invited Carl to my house," she said. "I don't talk to the group about my personal life. I don't know how he knew about Mary. None of it makes any sense. How could he have been lurking in my life without me knowing?" The notion sent chills over her skin. Could they be wrong? Could the killer be someone else, and her hope of holding Lily again soon was in vain? "What's wrong?"

Trees and traffic whipped past the window, blurring in a seasonal smear of orange and gold, dotted with irrelevant vehicles and the occasional pedestrian.

"Talk to me, West," she pushed. "Something's bothering you and you have to tell me what it is. I don't think my heart can take any more bad news or surprises."

West flicked his heated gaze her way. "I had him, and I let him go." He flexed and tightened his grip on the steering wheel. "I should've listened to my instinct and taken him to the station for questioning right then. I should've kept him there until I could prove he was the shooter."

Tina stared. In all the years they'd known one another, she had never been the rock he needed. Their relationship had always been a series of her crisis and his comfort. Though she'd never given him all the facts, he'd kept open arms for her. Never pushing, and never needing her strength in return. She was the victim. He was the hero.

Yet, here he was, opening up to her. Admitting his feelings of failure and frustration.

He shot a look her way. His handsome face scrunched in turmoil.

"You had nothing to go on," Tina blurted, praying her training would kick in while her mind scrambled to appreciate the new change between them. "Carl was behaving oddly, but being strange isn't against the law. Assault is, by the way, so you can't go unleashing a lifetime of pent-up frustration on him. He's not worth losing your career or ruining a thirty-year track record of good choices."

"I didn't always make the right choice." West gave her an apologetic look, and reached for her hand on the seat between them. "You're right. I did the best I could with the information I had. Now that I know Carl's behind this, I won't let him go a second time." He gave her a closer look. "How are you holding up?"

"I'm terrified," she admitted. "I feel half paralyzed with fear of all the unknowns. Part of me wants to leap from the car when we get there and tear the door down to get to her, but the rest of me is just really frightened. We don't know if we're right about Carl, and it makes me afraid of the letdown if she isn't there. If we're right, and she is there, I have no idea what condition I'll find her in. Sure, he might plan to make a happy family, but that doesn't mean he knows how to care for her. Does he even know how to prepare her bottles? Did he remember to buy formula? What if he got tired of her crying and..." A lump formed in her throat, silencing the words. "My mind has conjured the absolute most unthinkable scenarios. Whatever we find can't be worse than the things I've thought."

West's cell phone rang in his pocket, and he freed it as they hit the county road at full speed. "It's Deputy Loman," he said before swiping the screen to life. "Garrett," he answered. "You're on speaker with Tina Ellet."

"Are you en route to the Morgan home?" Loman asked.

"We are. I just hit the county road."

"ETA?" the deputy asked.

West's serious expression turned sour. "Maybe five minutes. Why?"

Tina's nails bit into the tender flesh of her palm. Her stomach rolled against her spine. The hope that had carried her from the hospital to the cruiser was suddenly gone. Eviscerated by the tone of the deputy's voice and expression on West's face.

"What's going on, Loman?" West growled.

"He's not here, Sheriff," the deputy responded. "No one's here. No truck. No baby. No Carl Morgan."

The No Trespassing signs posted at the end of Carl's drive appeared in the distance, and West pressed the gas pedal harder before slowing at the gravel drive.

Tina collapsed forward, sucking in shallow breaths and trying not to pass out. Her baby was there. She had to be. That was why they'd come. She could practically feel the weight of her in her arms again, and smell the shampoo on her sweet head. She was losing her all over again.

West rocked the vehicle to a stop and released a few venomous curses.

She forced herself upright with a guttural moan.

The deputy's cruiser sat outside her window.

West rounded the car's hood. A man in uniform waited on Carl's porch, hands on hips.

She watched in disbelief as West tried the trailer's front door and peeked in every window before circling the home and returning to the deputy for a hand-shake and departure.

He climbed back behind the wheel, already on his cell phone. The device now pressed to his ear. "Where are we on the warrant?" he asked. "I want into that trailer. Now. Loman's keeping watch in case Carl comes back."

Carl's trailer grew smaller in the distance as West reversed down the narrow drive, erasing Tina's hope of holding Lily again today. "Why are we leaving?" she asked. "I don't understand." She swiped a deluge of tears from her cheeks. "Why aren't we waiting for him to come home?"

"Loman's staying. I'm going to find Carl's closest neighbor."

Tina gripped the dash for stability as the cruiser spun back onto the county road in a shower of loose gravel and mud. Her body ached with a void where Lily belonged. She cradled her center with a weak, desperate arm.

She'd counselled her baby's kidnapper for more than a year without a single clue about what he had planned for her family. West blamed himself for what was happening, when in truth this was her fault. She should've seen Carl for what he was and stopped him. Instead, she'd assumed he had a rough past to work through. She'd thought he would open up eventually. If she was patient. If she didn't push. Now, she just wondered if Carl had ever needed her help at all. How much of what he'd let her see was even real? And why hadn't she been able to tell the difference?

Tina had failed her job as mother and therapist.

Now, her poor baby was in the clutches of a madman, and no one had any idea how to find her.

Chapter Eleven

West jammed his brakes and skidded to a stop near an elderly woman checking her mailbox at the edge of the winding road. Her eyes went wide at the sight of the sheriff's cruiser tossing gravel into the trees and over the berm. He crammed the gearshift into Park and turned to Tina. "Wait here."

The woman stepped back as he approached.

West tapped a finger to the brim of his hat. "Morning, ma'am. I'm West Garrett, Cade County Sheriff, and I have a few questions about the man who lives down the road about a quarter mile. His name's Carl Morgan. Do you know him?"

She narrowed her milky eyes on West and cocked her head. "I don't make a habit of gossiping."

"It's not gossip. A little girl's gone missing, and I think Carl Morgan has her, but he's not home. You'd be assisting in an investigation."

She shifted her gaze to Tina in the cab. "I don't know anything." She cleaned out her mailbox and turned to walk away.

"Wait!" Tina's door flew open, and she ran for the

old woman. "Please," she pleaded. "My name is Tina Ellet. I was in the parking lot with my patients yesterday when one man was shot and killed. Did you hear about that? Did you see that on the news?"

The woman straightened. A gleam of recognition lit her face. "I remember you. They play that clip every few minutes. Your daughter's missing. I know because there's an Amber Alert, and they play that, too."

Tina seemed to shrink at the sound of her words. "Please help me."

The woman's weary expression faded into something kind and motherly. "I'm Celia Hickman." She extended a hand to Tina, who shook it gratefully. "My husband knows more about Carl than I do. Carl keeps to himself."

"Thank you," Tina said, breaking the handshake and stuffing her fingers into her pockets.

Celia motioned for them to follow her up the lane, and Tina matched her pace.

West brought up the rear, keeping watch on the woods around them.

"Celia?" A man in bib overalls rocked in a chair on the porch. He planted his boots on the floor and sat taller at the sight of them.

"That's my husband, Frank," she told Tina. "These folks want to know about the neighbor," she called to her husband.

"Neighbor?" Frank struggled to stand. His gray beard and hair fluttered in the growing breeze. He unhooked a cane from the porch railing and met them in the yard. "Everything okay?"

A small, ratty-looking dog pranced into view. It gave a dismissive bark before retreating, uninterested.

West offered the man a hand. "Sir, I'm Sheriff Garrett."

"Sure you are," Frank answered. "I knew your daddy. You look just like him."

West forced a smile. "We have reason to think your neighbor, Carl Morgan, was involved in a series of crimes yesterday." He rested a palm on Tina's shoulder. "We think he has her daughter."

Frank's expression fell. "He said he was babysitting."

"What?" West asked. "When? Did you see the baby?"

The women turned on Frank with wide eyes and slack jaws. Shock jolted from Celia, and hope rose in waves from Tina.

"Frank," Celia screeched. "You didn't tell me he had a baby over there! I could've called the police."

"Well." Frank stroked his beard, looking a bit frightened. "I didn't see the baby. I only heard it, and I didn't think nothing of it anyway. Babysitting is babysitting." He swung his attention back to West. "The dog took off last night, and I tracked him all the way over to Carl's trailer. Dog was on Carl's porch barking up a storm. I got there at about the same time Carl came outside to complain. I apologized, tucked the mutt under my arm and said good-night. Then I heard the baby crying."

Tina clutched her hands to her chest. Terror bleached her face. "Was she okay?"

Frank looked past her to West. "I don't know. I didn't see her. He said he was babysitting for the night, then taking the little one home first thing in the morning."

Tina seemed to age before West's eyes. "Could they be at my house? Waiting?"

West worked the cell phone from his pocket and tapped the screen. "I'll ask Blake to get over there." He refocused on Frank and Celia. "Is there anything else you can tell us?"

"Afraid that's all." Frank frowned at Tina. "I know you probably don't think you should, miss, but you ought to lie down before you fall over." He shot West a pointed look. "She's not well."

West wound one arm around Tina's back and nodded. "Thank you. If you think of anything else, please call the sheriff's department. Tell them what you remember. They'll see to it that I get the message."

Celia leaned into Frank's side and rested her head on his chest. "We're going to be praying for you and your baby girl," she said.

Tina coiled in on West, releasing silent sobs against his ribs as they made their way back down the lane to his cruiser.

TINA WANDERED BACK to the cruiser, guided by West's strong arms. She'd done plenty of wrong things in her life. She probably deserved the pain and heartache she was feeling, but Lily didn't. Lily was pure and innocent and perfect. Why was this happening to her? Tina had no idea what her baby was going through, but whatever it was, she deserved better.

West zoomed through town toward her neighborhood, honking at intersections and waving apologetically at folks with gaping mouths. He arrived outside her home in half the time it would've taken to get there legally. Maybe there was a rule breaker under his perfect, upright facade. Or maybe the last twenty-four hours were wearing away everyone's composure.

Blake and two men in navy FBI windbreakers stood beside a large black SUV in her drive. No sign of the red pickup truck anywhere.

West charged forward to meet his brother and the other men.

Tina bumbled along on unsteady legs. Why weren't the agents inside? Where was Lily?

"No one's here," Blake announced. "Windows and doors are locked. Perimeter's secure."

Tina fell back a step. "He told his neighbors he was taking her home."

Blake offered a sad smile. "Wasn't his home. Wasn't yours."

West turned in a slow circle. "What do we know about Carl Morgan? Who are his people? Where else might he consider home?"

Tina collapsed onto the bottom porch step. Defeated. Drained of hope for the second time in an hour. "He moved here to be with his mom when she went into the assisted living facility."

Blake nodded. "We talked to her. She's got no love

for her son. Says he's a thorn in her side. Always has been. Never happy. Always acting out."

West looked to Blake. "Any word from his hometown police department?"

"Yeah." Blake braced his hands over his hips. "I got ahold of them on my way here. They had a file on the mom, nothing on Carl, but he was in the older reports. As a minor, he was present at the time of multiple police calls to the home. Mostly noise complaints by neighbors with an occasional drunk and disorderly for Mom. Home conditions were described as cramped and unclean. Neighbors speculated abuse and neglect, but I don't have any arrests to back that up." He angled his back to Tina. "I sent some men around last night to ask her neighbors about the truck you saw. I didn't get anything concrete."

West folded his arms. "Cole added the vehicle description and Carl's photo to the Amber Alert. He can't get far with this kind of coverage. Folks are going to recognize him, and someone's going to turn him in." He gripped the back of his neck. "I read all the reports and findings last night."

"Dead ends," Blake said.

"Yeah. Any chance Carl kept the family home in Pine Hurst? Maybe that's where he went."

"Nope," Blake answered. "Sold to pay for the nursing home."

"Right." West turned to face Tina. "I think you should talk to the neighbors. They know you. They're going to be more at ease talking to you than to some federal agent. Maybe if they're really trying to help, something useful will shake loose."

Blake dipped his chin. "Agreed. I can be intimidating."

Tina tried to laugh, but the sound was lost to despair. "I'll do it."

Blake turned toward his vehicle. "I'll reach out to the Pine Hurst Police Department again."

West took Tina's hand. "And check on the warrant. We need inside that trailer."

Tina moved beside him on numb legs, the late morning chill seeping into her bones. Her heart was empty, as hollowed out as the jack-o'-lanterns on her neighbors' doorsteps.

West rang the doorbells one by one. He explained the horrific situation to every homeowner on her street, while Tina stood dumbly at his side. She'd begun to disconnect from the day, from the pain. Her emotions pulled back, shut down to protect her. The tingling in her limbs was dreamlike, as if she might soon wake up from the nightmare. The neighbors' faces blurred into one abstract frown.

They moved methodically along her street. Up one side, then down the other, collecting the same information. Everyone had heard the truck last night. No one had gotten a look at the driver or the license plate. No one knew if her baby was in the vehicle.

"This isn't working," Tina said as they climbed the steps to the last house on her block. "We have to do something else."

West rang the bell and waited, tapping his palms

against his thighs. "We're planting seeds. That's important. If nothing else comes from this, you'll at least have reinforced your home with a personal neighborhood watch. One that's educated about the situation and aware of what to do if they see something unusual happening at your place. If Carl comes back here, we're guaranteed to hear about it now."

A moment later, the door opened several inches, and a woman Tina knew as Darcy peeked out. "Yes?" Darcy was a young mother of two. She had a husband who mowed the lawn and chased their kids through the sprinklers all summer. They seemed like a nice family, but they'd never spoken to Tina.

Tina edged around West, finally finding her voice. "Darcy?" Humiliation swirled in her gut. Tina didn't have a husband or a partner of any kind in this. She was Lily's only protector, and she'd failed her. "I'm Tina. I live across the street. This is Sheriff Garrett. Can we talk to you?"

Darcy gave West a long look, then pulled the door open and motioned them inside. "I thought you looked familiar."

West gave a limp smile. "How are the kids?"

"Good. Napping."

Tina held her questions. It was a small town. Of course they'd come across people who knew West and his family.

Darcy led them to the kitchen, where plastic toys peppered the floor and dry cereal dotted the table beside brightly colored bowls. "You have to excuse the mess. I wasn't expecting company."

"It's fine." Tina forced the words through gently chattering teeth. Excess adrenaline and stress were leaking from her in every form. She'd fallen asleep just before dawn, certain today would be better, but she was wrong. Yesterday was packed with shocking news, but there was still hope. Today, her hopes had been repeatedly crushed. Her heart along with them.

West took a seat at the cluttered table and dusted a space in front of him with one hand. "Darcy dated one of my brothers a while back," he announced. "Blake?"

"Ryder," she corrected.

"Right." West nodded.

Tina tried to control her expression, which was surely twisting into anger. She didn't care who Darcy dated. She cared where her baby was.

West tapped his cell phone to life and turned the screen to Darcy, as he had to every neighbor before her. "Do you recognize this man?"

"Sure." She cast a curious look at Tina.

Tina blinked. "You know him?"

"No." Darcy dragged the word out for several syllables. "I don't, but I recognize him. I've seen him at your place a bunch of times. I thought you two were a thing. Or related."

"Related?" West asked.

"Yeah. I started seeing him after your husband…" She trailed off, a look of remorse on her brow. "After the funeral, there were lots of folks coming and going. Bringing you food and looking after you. I assumed he was one of them. He came a lot. Addison had colic then, and I'd pace the house all day and night, hoping he'd fall asleep and wouldn't disturb the neighbors."

West leaned across the table. "Have you ever seen him go inside?"

"No. I don't think so. I've seen him go around the house, and I've seen him leave flowers." She shifted her gaze to Tina. "That's why I thought you two might be dating."

West's expression crumbled in disbelief. "He gave you flowers?"

"No," Tina protested. "Of course not."

Darcy scoffed. "He did. I saw him do it plenty of times. Big wildflower bouquets." She mimed the size with her hands. "I had the kids out in a stroller one morning after your baby was born. Everyone on the block had gone to work, and he was there. He saw me looking, so I told him how much I admired the flowers. He said they were a surprise, so I shouldn't tell. I swear I had no reason to think that was weird. I thought it was kind of sweet." She let her lids fall shut. "I should've known."

"You couldn't have known," West interrupted. "Did he say anything else? Anything at all."

Darcy reopened her eyes. "I asked how you two met, and he said you bought him a coffee when he needed it most. He said he knew then that you understood him, so he joined your group, and the two of you became quite close."

Tina's stomach dropped. "I always pay for the car behind me at the Cup of Life drive-through. Is that what he meant?" She replayed Darcy's words. "Oh, my goodness. Carl was following me before he joined my group? Everything he's told me was a lie." Tina pressed a cool palm to her burning face. "Buying coffee for strangers is an act of kindness. That's all." She cast her gaze at West. Her lips began to tremble. "He's stalking me because I was kind when he needed kindness, and this is my punishment."

West took her hand in his and squeezed. "Do you remember getting wildflowers?"

Words lodged in her throat. Images of the beautiful arrays burst through her mind. She'd loved the wildflowers. Even looked forward to them. "I received the first bundle on the day of Thomas's funeral. I get them every month now."

Darcy leaned against her counter. "Are you telling me I stood there with my kids and talked to a killer?"

Tina rolled her eyes up to meet Darcy's. "I'm sorry."

West tugged her hand in his. "Was there ever a card with the flowers? Did you keep it?"

"No," Tina answered. "Never. They were just flowers." Her tongue stuck to the roof of her mouth as all the facts of the day snapped into place, like a sick, demented puzzle. "He's been stalking me all this time. Through my pregnancy. All through Lily's life. I feel sick."

Darcy sprung away from the counter. She pointed around the corner, beyond heaping baskets of unfolded laundry. "Bathroom is opposite the laundry room."

Tina darted inside and pressed her forehead to

the door. She'd been violated, deceived and plotted against for more than a year by someone who wanted to steal everything she'd worked all her life to earn. And why? Because she'd bought him coffee? She wanted to scream. To cry. To crawl into bed and let the heavy sheet of darkness, now nipping at her conscience, pull her under and take her away.

"No." She smacked her palms against the door and went to splash cold water over her burning face. She stared at her haggard reflection. *I will find my baby*, she vowed.

And she knew what she needed to do next.

She needed to talk to Carl's mother.

Chapter Twelve

West scanned the lot outside the assisted living center in town. The sun had finally gotten a grip on the day, drying puddles and dew from the roads and grass. No signs of Carl, Lily or the red Ford pickup.

Tina popped her door open and headed for the building in long, purposeful strides.

"Wait." West caught her wrist in his hand and stopped her progress. "Slow down. You can't go in there hot, pouring everything we know out for her inspection and demanding answers. We don't know what kind of relationship Carl has with his mother, or if she's as strange as he is. Take a breath."

Tina pulled free. Something new and feral burned in her eyes. "That woman's son has my daughter. What do you want me to do? Play coy? Make small talk while he holds her hostage?"

"No." He planted his feet and dragged her to him, until her heart raged against his own. "I want you to remember Carl spent more than a year planning this. You need to choose your words carefully. Don't tell her more than she already knows from watching the news. If she has any information beyond that, we'll know it came from Carl." He rubbed his forehead, hoping it wasn't a complete mistake to bring Tina on this interview. He'd hoped her presence would add emphasis and encourage Carl's mother to share, but Tina's heated state of mind could do more harm than good. She needed to pull it together before she ruined the potential lead.

Tina made it to the welcome desk first and asked to see Mrs. Morgan.

The receptionist shook her head. "I'm sorry. We don't have a Mrs. Morgan here. There's a Mr. Morgenstern."

West pushed himself into the small space beside Tina. "Hello. I'm Cade County Sheriff West Garrett. We'd like to talk to Ms. Baxter."

Her wide brown eyes opened impossibly farther. "She's in suite three twelve."

"Thank you." West led the way to the room, taking long, purposeful strides and noting the exits. "Here it is."

"How did you know she had a different last name?" Tina asked.

West smiled. "Late-night reading."

The warm, buttery scent of fresh baked rolls clung to the air outside her door. A sign for the cafeteria pointed to the end of the hall. According to West's watch, and his gut, the time was nearing noon, and he'd already missed breakfast. West ignored the pang of hunger and knocked on the door. "Ms. Baxter?"

A woman in a hot-pink sweat suit answered. Long

gray hair hung to her narrow waist and slippers covered her feet. "Who are you?"

"I'm West Garrett, ma'am, and this is Tina Ellet. We're friends of your son."

She opened the door, then headed for a small couch pushed against the wall and picked up her remote control. The room was decorated like a tiny dorm room. Bed. Mini fridge. Love seat and television. Small, homey items lined the walls and every flat surface. She poked the remote into the air like a sword, at a television mounted high on the opposite wall. "Carl doesn't have any friends. You're here like the others this morning, hoping I'll turn him in."

West worked his jaw. This trip suddenly felt like another dead end. A frustrating one. "We have reason to believe Carl shot a man in cold blood yesterday, then kidnapped an infant." The civility in his tone was failing.

She stopped channel surfing and flicked her gaze quickly to him. The Amber Alert for Lily lodged firmly in the corner of the television. Carl's face was posted side by side with one of a baby wearing a pink quilted jacket.

Ms. Baxter powered the television off.

Tina froze near the coffee table, where a mass of wildflowers erupted from a stout vase. "Did Carl give you these?"

Ms. Baxter rolled her eyes. "Yeah. He comes here all the time, trying to make up for all the trouble he caused me growing up."

"Growing up in Pine Hurst?" Tina asked.

The woman shot her a sour face. "I don't have to answer your questions. You think Carl did those things, then you figure it out. Leave me out of it."

Tina moved cautiously toward the love seat. "Carl brings me flowers like this, too."

West locked his jaw against a number of rude clarifications. He pretended, instead, to examine a collection of photos taped to the closet door. Blake told him this was a dead end.

"So, you're the girlfriend?" Ms. Baxter laughed. The raspy sound turned quickly into a deep and uncontrollable cough that took more than a minute to quiet and another to recover from. She lifted a glass of water from the table to her lips; a tremor wobbled the liquid inside her glass. Eventually, she turned her ashen face back to Tina. "He wasn't lying. You are pretty. He says you're a doctor."

"I'm a clinical psychologist," Tina corrected.

Ms. Baxter made a deep throaty noise that led to another, less aggressive, round of coughing. "Figures. I told him no doctor would want him."

"Why not?"

The woman crinkled her nose in distaste. "Why not? Have you met him? He practically flunked out of high school. Was rejected for the military. Makes no money. He barely talks, and when he does it's with a st-t-t-tutter," she mocked. "He was always a mama's boy."

"How so?" West asked, unable to stay out of it any longer.

"He stayed inside all the time, clinging to my hip.

Worrying about me. Fussing over me. 'You drink too much. Don't smoke. That man's not nice to you.'" She mimicked her son in a whiny childlike voice. "He didn't like fighting or hunting or sports or getting dirty. All I had to do was yell a little and he'd run off. Anytime I hit him, he'd hide under the bed like a damn injured dog. Don't think I didn't try to make a man of him. I had plenty of boyfriends who tried to toughen him up, but it never took. Even dated a cop once." She gave West a pointed look. "Didn't matter. Carl just curled into a sad little ball and did nothing with his life. He spent more time with those wildflowers than he ever did with any woman."

"Carl needs help," Tina whispered, "and so does my baby."

Ms. Baxter looked her over. "He only likes you because you bought him coffee. Just like that little girl with the lemonade stand. Any woman so much as looks his way and he's falling over himself to love her. Ridiculous. If women wanted pets, they'd buy a dog."

"What happened to the little girl with the lemonade stand?" West asked, suddenly worried that Carl had a lifetime of missing women in his wake.

Ms. Baxter scoffed. "She broke his heart. What do you think happened to her? Then I poured that lemonade over his head and told him to be a man! No woman was ever going to love a weak, clingy cupcake like him."

This was getting them nowhere. West hated to admit it, but that was exactly what Blake said had happened to his men when they visited her earlier.

He'd failed to mention, however, that she was a mean, spiteful old woman. He couldn't imagine being raised by someone so hurtful and vindictive. No wonder Carl was warped. Whatever was wrong with him may or may not have been there from the day he was born, but living with Ms. Baxter certainly couldn't have helped matters. He widened his stance and set a hand on Tina's shoulder, hoping to offer her a bit of his strength when hers was clearly wearing thin. "This kid sounds like a real thorn in your side. Why not tell us what you know so we can punish him for what he's done?"

Her eyes flashed hot. "Because he's mine and you can't have him."

Well, that solidified it. She was as insane as her son. "Any idea where he'd go with a baby? He told a neighbor he was taking her home."

She shrugged, attention glued to West's hand on Tina. "Like I said. You're the detective. You figure it out."

"Ms. Baxter, if you know where he is and intentionally withhold that information, you can be charged with aiding and abetting."

She stuck her wrists out. "What are you gonna do? Haul me in for protecting my son? Take me from this prison and lock me in another one?" Her voice grew louder with each word, and she began to cough. "If he took that baby, it wouldn't surprise me."

A nurse poked her head through the open door. "Everything okay in here, Ms. Baxter?"

"No," the old woman choked out between coughs. "These two are pissing me off."

The nurse looked to West. "Sir," she started.

West waved a hand. "We're leaving, but we'll be back, so make sure Ms. Baxter doesn't go anywhere." He wrapped a protective arm around Tina and guided her back through the building, the woman's cough echoing down the hall behind them.

TINA FELL ONTO West's couch. Thankful to be somewhere she could lie down, and equally guilty for wanting to rest at a time like this. What was wrong with her to think of such a thing when her daughter was missing? Was Lily able to sleep? Was she cold? Hungry?

Tina forced her eyes wider and gave her cheeks a few sharp pats.

West's stomach growled loudly for the tenth time since they'd arrived at the assisted living facility. "Are you hungry?" he asked. "Because I need to eat something before we have to take off again."

"I think toast or crackers is all I can manage," she said.

West opened a cupboard, then tossed a sleeve of saltines across the room to her. "Anything else?"

She snorted. "Water or coffee. Probably coffee." Her body felt fifty pounds too heavy. Even keeping her head upright had become a chore on the ride back to West's home. She situated herself on the couch so that she could watch West in the kitchen. It was hard to fit the man before her into the context of high school sweetheart. The angles of his face were sharper, his voice a little deeper and his heart was still as big as ever, but he wasn't a kid anymore. Odd to think that while she was away becoming an adult, he'd been doing the same and she'd missed it.

He busily unloaded the contents of his fridge onto the counter and arranged it all in layers on a hoagie bun until he had the equivalent of a Scooby-sized sandwich. "What'd you think of sweet little Ms. Baxter?" he asked, sarcasm dripping from the words.

Tina peeled the cracker sleeve open and pursed her lips. She'd been plagued by a terrible thought since meeting the angry woman who showed no love or concern for her son. "I think Carl wants me to replace her."

West froze. A horrified look screwed over his face. "He wants you to be his mother?"

"No, but I think he wished someone had been." She took her time trying to find the right words for what she thought was happening. The visit with Carl's mother was extremely disturbing. And eye-opening. "I think he wants a woman in his life to be the mother he never had. I don't think he wants me to *be* his mother, as much as he wants me to be *a* mother who belongs to him. She said this all goes back to the coffee I bought him, and the little girl who'd done something similar when he was younger. When I gave him the coffee, he attached himself to the kindness of a woman. As awful as his mother is to him, they were new here over a year ago, and their already broken dynamic was changing. She's sick. If he's going to lose her, he'd better be prepared. Then, he watched me go through a pregnancy and care for a newborn. The kind of woman he wished his mother had been literally become a mother."

"He wants a normal family," West said, wiping a dollop of mustard from the corner of his lip.

"I think so. Unfortunately, that's not in the cards for everyone." Herself included. "It scares me because he's hobbling a family together, thinking it's all going to be glorious, but this situation can't possibly live up to his expectations, and he'll be angry all over again. The failure of his efforts will exacerbate his feelings of inadequacy, and he'll need to be rid of us, so he can try again."

West watched her for several long beats. "He doesn't have you."

Tina stared at the cracker pinched between her fingertips. "No, but he has Lily, and that's the same thing."

"It's not the same to him. You're the endgame here."

Tina set the crackers aside and scooted forward on the couch cushion. She curled her fingers around the edge and refocused her attention on West. It was time to share her crazy idea with him. "We need to find him so I can go with him. Then I can be sure Lily's okay and try to get her away from him."

"First of all, no," West said. "Absolutely not. And second of all, we *will* find him. After that, we'll take him down. We will *not* turn you over."

Tina bit her tongue. If West could arrest Carl without Lily being harmed in the process, fine. But if things went south, and she saw an opportunity to save her baby, that's exactly what she'd do. Regardless of the risk. Protecting Lily was all that mattered.

Chapter Thirteen

Tina hovered over her third cup of coffee and waited for West's phone to ring. He'd insisted on working from his laptop, instead of hitting the road again, and they'd already been sitting still for more than an hour. If it was up to Tina, she'd knock on every door in Cade County until someone recognized Carl's picture.

She'd already tried and failed to rest, despite the glaring physical effects of sleep deprivation. Images of Lily's sweet face flashed repeatedly into her mind, only to morph quickly into red-faced cries of desperation. Tina's nerves were shot, and every precious memory of her baby was slowly becoming twisted in her absence. Was Lily hurt? Was she cold? Sick? Scared? Was she hungry? Was she being changed and fed? Did he have formula for her? Did he know how many ounces to feed her?

Tina ground the heels of her hands against her sore and puffy eyes. She tipped her head from side to side, stretching the bunched-up muscles of her neck and shoulders. Her limbs were heavy and slow to respond when she wanted to move. Worst of all, the ceaseless worry had sent her on a downward spiral of emotional states. Most recently, she'd passed from heart-wrenching desperation into complete detachment. West was kind enough to pretend not to notice. One minute she was in mental hell, and the next minute there was a void where all her internal suffering had been. The seemingly endless tears and tormented thoughts had simply vanished. Her mind was blank. Her emotional capacity stunted. When she tried to think of the horrible things she'd been dwelling on, her mind simply rejected them. The whole thing was unsettling, but she couldn't seem to change it.

She set the empty mug aside and forced herself upright. "Care if I use your shower while you do whatever it is you're doing?"

West pulled his eyes from the laptop screen. "I'm reviewing reports taken by my men and Blake's. Hoping something will stand out." He curled his mouth into a smile that didn't reach his eyes. "Go ahead. Take your time. If I find anything useful while you're in there, I'll come knocking."

"Thanks." Tina headed for West's room, where she'd left her overnight bag, trying not to think of some more pleasant reasons he might interrupt her shower.

The scalding water did nothing to snap her out of her stupor. She slid to the shower floor and drew her knees to her chest, letting the water flow over her, wishing for her sense of self to return. This was the perfect time for a breakdown. She had privacy and white noise to drown the cries, hot water to mask the tears and explain the flush of her skin. Unfortunately, her tears seemed to have dried up with her emotions. The detachment she felt was textbook self-protection, but she hated it. She'd met dozens of people in therapy who spent all their energy trying not to feel, but that wasn't who she was. Tina normally felt everything. For everyone. Her heart ached for strangers' losses and rejoiced with their victories. Neighbors. Friends. People on television shows and commercials. Tina lived with enough emotion to power the universe, and she'd never seen it as a burden. It meant she was human.

She gave up on the shower and toweled off. She powered up her travel blow-dryer and wiped a hole in the steam on West's bathroom mirror. So far, he hadn't knocked. Which meant there was no news on Lily or the monster who'd stolen her. She'd give anything to know where they were right now, and how she could get to them, but Carl had never said much about his present circumstances. When he had opted to talk in therapy, which wasn't often, he'd focused on stories from his childhood. Instances that had hurt or angered him. He'd vaguely discussed his mother's insensitivity and the harshness of her boyfriends without saying anything substantial. He'd nodded along as others group members recalled being beaten or locked in rooms, humiliated and taunted, but Carl had never given any indication of where he might go under duress.

Re-dressed in yoga pants and a fitted, long-sleeve top, she tied her hair into a messy bun and went back to sit on the couch, where she would presumably stay until something motivated West to leave.

He gave a double take when she walked in, blinking sharp blue eyes before turning back to his computer and setting it aside. "Feel any better?"

"Cleaner."

"Refreshed?"

"Sure." She pulled her feet up on the couch and reopened the cracker sleeve. Might as well get a little something in her stomach while she wasn't too nauseated to eat.

He narrowed his eyes. "Anything I can do for you?"

"Actually." She squared her shoulders and dusted crumbs from her palms.

West swiveled to face her fully, curiosity clinging to his handsome features. "What?"

"I'm not one to talk about my personal baggage," she began.

West made a sarcastic expression. "That is brand-new information."

She rolled her eyes. She also wasn't one to feel detached from herself, but that was exactly what was happening. Being with West helped. She had never spent a second with him and not felt something. Her chest was already beginning to swell and tingle. She was coming back to herself just by speaking to him. "What you don't know is that I don't talk about those things because I can never find the right words. The stuff that has weighed me down since we first met was so much bigger and more complicated than I

could describe that I kept it inside. I pushed it down."
Tina paused. This wasn't an easy conversation, and
maybe the timing was awful, but at least she was beginning to feel again, and if she wasn't numb, then
maybe she'd be okay. "I pretended my home life didn't
affect me, but it did. It was unbearable, so I looked
for ways to enjoy the other parts of my life. I tried to
pretend the rest wasn't real. I should have told you a
long time ago. I'm sorry I didn't, but I'd like to tell
you now."

Her words seemed to pull the humor from West's
face. He fixed her with those soulful eyes and waited.

She'd mentally rehearsed this conversation for
years. So, why now, when the opportunity was before her, did she want to run away? She worked the
fabric of her shirt's hem between her fingers. "My
dad was horrible. To me. To Mom. To everyone. He
was abusive verbally, emotionally, physically." She
peeked up at him for a response.

There was fresh hurt in West's eyes. "I could've
protected you."

"We were in high school, West. No, you couldn't.
No one could."

"I could have. We were young, but what we had
was powerful. If we'd stayed together, nothing he did
would have mattered."

Tina felt a guttural roar building in her center.
"You think his behavior didn't matter?" It didn't affect them? Was he kidding? Maybe the town didn't
know as much about what went on behind the Ellet
doors as she'd thought. "My dad hurt us. Can you un-

derstand that? My mom got the worst of it, but I was ruined. He shamed us, belittled us, denied us every single thing we needed from food to affection. He drank up all his paychecks, when he bothered to hold a job long enough to get one. He blamed us when he couldn't. He blamed Mom for everything, and she took it lying down. Literally. And I—I was alone. And broken."

West inched closer with an unfathomable expression. "You were never alone."

Her skin crawled with humiliation. She hated baring herself to anyone, particularly her worst self, and especially to him. "Forget it."

"Hey," he said carefully. "I get why you wanted out of that house, even out of town, but it didn't mean we couldn't be together. You didn't have to cut me off and act as if I'd never mattered. Like *we* hadn't mattered." His haunted expression teetered between regret and heartbreak. "I would've waited for you. For college. Whatever you needed to do. You knew that and you still left. You changed your number. Returned my letters. Why?"

She raised her hands in the air and let them drop lifelessly to her lap. "I had to." She batted stinging eyes. "I did it because I loved you and you deserved more. Something better. More honest and less toxic than what I was." She released a humorless laugh. "What I am."

He narrowed his eyes. "You're not toxic."

"Of course you don't think so. You refuse to see me for the mess that I am. I'm a train wreck waiting to happen. The people I love either hurt me, like Dad did, run from me, like Mom, or die, like Thomas."

"That's only three people, Tina, and it's not everyone who loved you. I loved you." He ground the words through his teeth, shredding her heart with each syllable. "I never left or ran away. Hell, I'm still right here where you left me ten years ago."

He'd loved her. Past tense. A long time ago. Another lifetime. She ignored the painful churning in her chest. She had to be logical and calm. Had to make him understand. "Look." She exhaled slowly and began again. "Do you think my parents started out all messed up and wasted? That one day, long ago, some young, drunk version of Dad saw a young depressed version of my mom, thought to himself, *I'd like to trash her life*, so he slapped her across the face, told her it was her fault that he never had anything nice and she married him?"

West recoiled.

"Every couple starts out happy," she said. "Young. In love. Hopeful. Even them, and look what happened. I didn't want to wind up like them, and I sure as heck wasn't going to drag you down with me."

He caught her hand in his and smoothed his palm against hers. "You aren't your mother, and I'm not your father. *We* are nothing like them."

"You're exactly like your dad," Tina argued. "Just like your brothers. Your uncles. I would expect you of all people to know that it's true what they say about apples not falling far from the tree."

West blew out a long, angry laugh. "I turned out

like my family because I chose to. It was my goal."
He pounded a fist to his chest. "I decided who I became. Just like you did."

Tina nearly choked on a sharp intake of breath. The
emotions that had been hiding away and making her
numb came back with a crushing blow. She wanted to
believe him, but she'd never seen herself the way West
had. Strong and independent. In control of herself and
her life. Those were just more things she wished were
true, but weren't. "If I decided how my life would turn
out, then why am I here like this now?" Her hands
balled into fists on her lap. She pulled them away from
him. "A madman, who I counseled—" she swallowed
back the cracker attempting to reemerge "—stole my
baby. He killed one of my patients."

"I know."

"Don't do that," she warned. "Don't try to smooth
this over. Not everything that goes wrong in the world
can be fixed with a little Garrett charm and a few
waves of your magic badge. I did this. I let Carl get
close to me, and I ruined everything I worked for
with my ignorance."

A crippling sense of loss flattened her will to fight,
and she fell into West's waiting arms. Pride demanded
she get up and walk away, but she couldn't bring herself to care about pride anymore. "All I ever wanted
to be was a good mother," she whispered against his
chest. "And I failed."

WEST FOLDED TINA against his chest. He hated the pain
she was in. Hated Carl for putting her through this

now, and her dad for everything he'd put her through before. Most of all, he hated himself for not telling her that he was the reason her mom had vanished.

He pulled in a deep breath and peered down at the top of her troubled head. "Tina." He cleared his throat, choosing his words carefully, despite the awful timing. If he didn't tell her soon, the truth would seem like something he'd intentionally kept from her, instead of something he'd hoped to bring up when they weren't in the middle of a crisis.

Tina twisted in his grip and stared back at him with wide, red-rimmed eyes. "Yeah?"

His phone buzzed on the table, halting the words on his tongue.

She shifted away from him, wiping her eyes against her sleeve. "What is it?"

"Hold that thought." West snatched the phone off the table and checked the text. His stomach soured at the stream of photos arriving in succession.

"What's wrong?" she asked, craning her neck for a better look at the unthinkable.

A small pink pacifier lay under the edge of a worn-out couch. The small plastic nub was speckled with dirt, dust and hair from the yellowed linoleum floor. "Blake and his men are inside Carl's trailer."

"Oh, God." Tina ran for the bathroom. Her retch was audible as West responded to the text. He'd accept that response as a positive ID of Lily's pacifier.

THEY RODE IN silence to Carl's place.

Tina had threatened to walk when West tried to

convince her to stay at his house until the search was completed. They'd compromised with her agreement to wait in the cruiser. As anxious as she was to get a look at the location where Lily had been held, the trailer was a crime scene and she was forbidden from entering. The best West could do was report back and share photos as he explored the space. Part of him was glad to have her there. Leaving her alone anywhere too long was a risk he wouldn't take.

He parked behind a line of cruisers and government vehicles filling the space between Carl's trailer and the county road. "Sit tight," he said. West climbed out, but waited for Tina to nod in agreement before closing the door.

He headed up the gravel lane in search of Blake. By the looks of it, all the Cade County deputies were aiding the search party, as well as a significant influx of federal agents. A bubble of pride puffed his chest.

Blake's FBI team crawled over the trailer in matching navy jackets with yellow block letters, shining black lights, snapping photos and bagging evidence. One agent dug through an overturned trash can beside the wooden porch. The putrid stench of spoiled food and loaded diapers peppered the air. West pressed one wrist against his burning nose. The agent's thin latex gloves and medical mask didn't seem like nearly enough protection.

West lifted his chin when Blake took notice of his approach. "What have we got?"

Blake braced his hands against his hips. "This

place is a pigpen. I don't know how anyone lives like that. I hate to think of what that baby went through."

West repositioned himself, forming a wall between Blake and his cruiser at the end of the driveway. As if he could somehow protect Tina from what was happening before him. Thankfully, she couldn't hear Blake's words.

"We've got dirty diapers and empty formula cans in the trash," Blake said. "There's paths everywhere. Boot prints and ATV tracks crisscross the whole property. I can't say for sure yet if the prints are Carl's or not. We're making casts of the impressions."

"What else?"

A line of hounds weaved their way through the surrounding underbrush, eagerly chasing scents on the breeze. West knew they weren't all trained to search for the living. He fought the blast of anxiety squeezing his chest. He wouldn't accept the possibility of finding Tina's daughter in an unthinkable condition.

"Well, wherever he went, he didn't take his bathroom stuff. So either he's planning to buy new, or he's planning to come back. The second one would be stupid, so I'm going with the first. We've flagged his credit cards and put his face on every form of news media. We will flush him out. It's only a matter of time. He can't go anywhere in three counties without someone recognizing him and that baby. We're expanding the Amber Alert as time goes on."

"What about the cadaver dogs? Tell me they're just doing their due diligence."

"For now, yes. I figured I'd get some out here with the search team. Cover all the bases. See what turns up. The trackers were given items from Tina's home to catch the baby's scent, and we pulled Carl's clothes from the trailer."

A flick of instinct pinched his gut. "How far have the search teams gone?"

"Not far. They're just getting started."

West turned in a small circle, scanning the surrounding hills and trees. Something felt off about the scene before him. "Did you head over here after the search warrant came in?"

"Nah. The neighbors called the station. Said you spoke with them earlier, and they could hear the baby crying again."

West twisted at the waist for a look over one shoulder. The Hickman's home was barely visible through the trees. Tina's silhouette was motionless inside his vehicle. He waved and waited. When she waved back, he sighed in relief. This whole case was getting to him. "Why didn't you call me after you spoke with them?"

Blake dragged his gaze over West from head to toe. "When was the last time you slept?"

"Last night."

"For how long?"

He glanced at Tina once more. West wasn't sure how long he'd slept, but it was probably longer than Tina, and he wasn't going to stop working this case until she had Lily back in her arms. She surely couldn't take much more of this. His heart was nearly torn in two and he'd never even met Lily. He couldn't imagine what Tina was going through. "I need you to keep me in the loop on this. All of it. I'll decide when I sleep. Got it?"

Blake sucked his teeth and stared. "Yep."

"Anything else you haven't told me?"

"No. How about you? Did you make a trip out to see Ms. Baxter like Tina suggested?"

West groaned.

Blake snorted. "She's a real piece of work, and her file's a mile long. No wonder her kid is messed up."

"I thought the same thing. I read the file. Didn't see anything on Carl, though. Means he's good. Smart. He's never been caught." West knew there was no way a guy went from being an upright citizen to a killer and child abductor in one day. He'd probably committed dozens of crimes over the years, all leading up to this. "Good news is he probably thinks he's untouchable. That means he'll get brave and stupid. When he does, I'm going to be there to…"

A sharp and sudden crack of gunfire echoed through the trees. The air rushed from West's chest as Blake plowed into him, smashing him against the wooden porch. Together, they rolled onto the muddied ground and ducked around the trailer's edge. A large hole splintered the boards just inches from where West had stood moments before.

The hounds went wild, barking and howling into the sky. The echoes of their laments soared through the hills as a dozen lawmen drew their weapons and took cover.

"West!" Tina's voice rushed into the mix. She ran in the trailer's direction, blind panic ravaging her face.

"Get down!" West launched himself toward her.

The next crack tore through his flesh. He'd no sooner heard the sound than felt the searing pain rip through his arm. A bulging rain barrel burst behind him with a loud snap. Water gushed onto the ground, splitting into rivers at his feet and slicking the already mushy earth.

West's hand flew to his wound on instinct. He dove back to where he'd come with a rampaging heart rate and blinding pain. "Get down," he called again, unable to reach Tina where she stood frozen in fear.

She swung her head toward the cruiser, then back to West, apparently torn between making a run for him or returning to the car, already several yards away. Her wide eyes locked on the blood flowing over his fingers where they wrapped his bicep.

"Now!" Blake barked at Tina. His voice was low and authoritative. "Move it!"

An irrational bout of anger rose in West's chest at the sound of his brother speaking to her that way.

She winced, but found her feet and ducked behind the nearest cruiser. She pressed her back to the tire and covered her head with both hands.

"You okay?" Blake asked West, attention trained on the hillside.

"Flesh wound." He peeled his fingers away and shook his jacket off for a better look. "Where's that nerd Cole when we need him?" Cole would know how to stop the blood in an instant. He'd know how serious the injury was, and how soon West could climb the hill and stop Carl Morgan.

"He'll be around in a minute," Blake answered, still searching the trees for signs of the shooter. "He can smell an injury six counties away."

West tried to tear his shirt across the hem and failed. The pain in his right arm kept it still at his side, and he couldn't do much with his left.

"I can't see a damn thing," Blake complained. He inched out from behind the trailer and sent a round into the woods.

No return fire.

Blake swore. "You know the nut is up there in camouflage with a rifle and a scope, laughing at us with our peashooters and no advantage."

West moved in the opposite direction from his brother, scanning the trees for a glint of sun off the rifle scope. "*We* aren't crazy. That's our advantage."

"Is it, though?" Blake deadpanned. "Because right now he's got us in a barrel, and we're working blind while he tries to kill you."

The words rang in West's ears.

Carl wasn't shooting at authorities for going through his trailer or interfering with his plan. He was trying to get rid of West like he had Steven from group therapy, and probably Tina's husband. West wouldn't be surprised if Carl had arranged this, intentionally allowing Lily to cry so the neighbors would make the call that brought him there.

The roar of an ATV engine echoed through the

hills. West squinted into the distance, struggling for a glimpse at the vehicle hidden behind a million red and gold leaves. "He's got an ATV. Just like the tracks you found." He pulled his grandpa's white handkerchief from one pocket and stretched it out in plain view of the hillside. He wiggled his fingertips, swinging the flag in surrender.

The engine's roar grew soft and distant as West repurposed his handkerchief from little flag to bandage, wadding and pressing it against the gunshot wound on his arm.

Hounds rushed into view on long red leashes tied to trainers' wrists, racing toward the disappearing sound.

Blake holstered his weapon, deflated. "He's gone." He marched toward the open trailer door, where an agent poked his head out. He ordered his team to stop what they were doing and look for fresh ATV tracks. "Find them, then follow them. We need to know where he's hiding."

West made a run for Tina. His head swam slightly with pain and adrenaline.

Cole appeared in the driveway, jogging straight for him with the medical supply bag he never left home without. "Sit down before you fall down, you moron," he scolded.

West chuckled, but kept moving. He must look like he felt.

He waved the nearest pair of deputies over in his direction. "Pull up an aerial view of this property. Find out what else is around here. There's got to be another building. An old barn. Abandoned home. Someplace he could hide a baby, a truck and an ATV." That would explain how he'd been able to disappear so quickly and thoroughly following the Amber Alert. Maybe he and Lily hadn't gone anywhere at all. Maybe they were still right there in Cade County waiting for the chance to kill West or take Tina.

He landed in the gravel at her side, and his men dispersed.

Tina clung to West's chest and kissed his cheek with fervor. "I thought I was about to lose you all over again."

Cole squatted beside them, pulling latex gloves over his hands and prepping his medic supplies.

West stroked her hair and placed a kiss against her head. "I'm not that easy to kill."

Cole cast a mischievous look in Tina's direction. "Believe me. I've tried."

West pulled her tighter and winced as Cole put pressure on the wound. Carl wasn't getting anywhere near Tina. Whatever his plan was, it was going to fail because the next time Carl Morgan came within striking distance, West would be ready.

Chapter Fourteen

Cole drove West to the hospital in his cruiser. Tina followed in West's, unapologetically running every light Cole did. He used sirens and flashers. Tina used a heavy hand and horn.

She locked the car and raced through the emergency room doors, desperate to see if West was still okay. That nothing had gone horribly wrong since she'd been forced to leave his side. Cole had insisted the wound was superficial, but the way he'd driven implied something more.

Tina scanned the nearly empty waiting area. No Cole. No West. Only half a dozen people in a room with three dozen chairs. Where were the Garretts? They'd only been a minute ahead of her.

The room swayed, and she forced herself to fight another brewing round of panic. She rubbed a hand against the pain in her chest as she approached the admittance desk. "There was a deputy," she told the nurse. "He came in right before me. The sheriff was with him. He had a gunshot wound to the arm." She slapped her bicep to clarify the injury location.

The nurse nodded. "Deputy and Sheriff Garrett. They never wait. They went right back and told me to send you ahead, as well." She lifted a pen in the direction of two swinging doors.

Tina broke into a sprint, trying not to think too long or hard about the nurse's words. *They never wait.* How often were they here? And why?

Her hands met the double doors with only one thing in mind. "West!"

The impact reverberated through her palms and wrists.

Locked.

A moment later, the barrier parted. Cole stepped into view, motioning her back. "Come on. He's fine. I was just on my way to meet you."

She followed him to a pale green curtain drawn around a bed and two silhouettes.

Tina darted through the flimsy veil. Her heart soared at the sight of the only man she'd ever truly loved. "West."

A doctor on a rolling chair jammed a curved metal needle into West's arm. He gave a tug and shot West a pointed look before tipping his head in Tina's direction. "She's with you?"

"That's right," West said, his voice low and scratchy. His cocky smile nearly made her grin. "She's with me."

The doctor pinched West's puckered skin and laced another round of suture thread through. His white lab coat dusted the stool where he worked, shifting over his thighs with each move of his blue-gloved hands. He paused for a longer look at Tina. "You hurt anywhere?"

"No." Her heart and lungs needed to be reminded regularly of their duties, but other than that? "I'm fine."

Cole planted a hand on her shoulder. "Let's get out of here so he can finish." He nudged her back. Away from West's side. "He'll be fine. Carl's rain barrel took the brunt of that shot."

Tina lifted a hand to West and the doctor, completely at a loss for words. Was it the lawmen in them that allowed them to speak so casually about things that crushed her lungs? She absently shook her head. Maybe it was the *Garrett* in them.

She followed Cole into the waiting room and fell onto a chair. "This is my fault."

"Yeah," Cole said sadly.

She jerked her head around to find the same goofy smile on Cole's face that West had worn a few minutes before. She dropped her head against the wall behind her chair. "What is wrong with you people? Your brother was shot. Why aren't you more upset?"

Cole took the seat at her side and placed one ankle over the opposite knee. "I don't know. Probably because he lived."

Tina groaned and sunk low in her seat. "He was shot."

Cole hooked his elbow over the arm of his chair. "I'm sorry about what's happening to you. No one's trying to make light of it. It's just our way of getting through. Gotta claim the victories, you know?

Today, Carl Morgan set us up so he could try to kill my brother, but he lost." He turned his hopeful face to hers and leveled her with the trademark Garrett stare. "It won't be the last time we beat him at his game. Yeah?"

She forced her swollen, sticky tongue to work. "Yeah."

"Good." Cole rolled onto one hip and freed his phone from his pocket. "It's Blake." He walked several paces away to take the call.

Tina twisted for a look at the motionless double doors separating her from West. She longed to return to him, or maybe sneak up on Cole and eavesdrop, but her legs felt like noodles. She refocused on the deputy, trying and failing to read his lips. His body language seemed at ease, maybe even disappointed, but his expression was stiff. Whatever had left him feeling let down, wasn't anything too concerning. Definitely nothing to do with her directly. He hadn't glanced her way once since taking the call.

"Ready?" West's voice sounded at her side.

She spun in her chair. "You're done?"

"Yep." He reached for her. The sleeve over his opposite arm was torn and dark with blood. "It's going to hurt like hell tomorrow. You okay to drive?"

She shrugged heavy shoulders. "I don't know. I guess I'm in better shape than you."

"Sold." He wound his good arm across her back.

"I can't believe I just watched you get shot."

He headed for the automatic doors. "You watched

me get grazed. That rain barrel was the one who got shot."

"Right. I almost forgot. You're perfectly fine," she deadpanned.

"Well, I mean, I am kinda bummed my jacket has a hole in it."

Tina released a heavy breath. The more she protested, the harder West would work to convince her there was nothing wrong. They'd done this dance before.

"Wait up!" Cole jogged to West's side before they reached the exit. "FBI tracked the ATV to a main road. They're running on the theory he used the truck to transport the ATV, but that road isn't regularly traveled. No cameras. Maybe he's staying nearby and using the ATV for transportation. No one's looking for him on a four-wheeler."

"What about the property?" West asked. "Any barns or other structures on the map?"

"No. The dogs and search team have finished walking the area. No additional buildings or shelters were found. They're moving into neighboring parcels now."

Tina watched as West processed the new information. His jaw clenched and popped. A vein pulsed in his temple. She wrapped herself tightly with trembling arms. "What about Lily?"

The men turned their eyes on her.

"Is he riding around on a four-wheeler with my infant? Or leaving her alone somewhere?" She pulled her shoulders up to her ears, fully ready to explode from the pressure in her heart. "If he's out joyriding and taking shots at the sheriff, then who's watching my baby?"

Cole tucked the phone back into his pocket and pulled out his keys. He gave Tina a sad smile.

No one knew. She understood that. But the concerns were valid, and she could only hope Lily was still alive to be watched at all.

Vomit rose in her throat.

Cole moved his full attention to West without responding. "Carl's trailer is sitting on a hunk of ground that isn't listed as his on the auditor's site, so I'm going to see what I can find out about the owner."

"Good idea," West said. "Maybe the owner can give us some insight. Emergency contact info, prior addresses, anything we don't already have on Morgan."

"I'll keep you posted." Cole saluted and left.

Tina touched West's fingers where they rested on her hip. "Can we check on Mary before we leave? I've been worried about her tests." She'd feel a lot better knowing Mary was healing, and that she wasn't any more injured than the doctors had originally suspected.

She'd also like to know if Mary had thought of anything else that could help them find her daughter.

"Sure." West dropped his arm from her waist and led her down the hallway toward an elevator bay. He leaned against the wall inside the car.

Tina scrutinized the blank cop expression on his face. His skin had lost its healthy glow. He was being brave for her sake. Even if he wasn't scared or worried, he was hurting. Just too stubborn to admit it. "You lost a lot of blood. You should eat and rest. I'll bet that's exactly what the doctor said before he let you go. Isn't it?"

West forced a weak smile. "The doctor said if I didn't get your number and ask you out, then he would."

She smiled. "Did not." Handsome as he had been, the doctor had seemed far more interested in West's injuries than in her.

"True," he admitted, "but when I saw him looking at you that way, I set him straight before he got any gutsy ideas."

Tina laughed. She gave West her most enticing smile, enjoying the unexpectedly flirtatious moment before life came at her again. "How was he looking at me exactly?"

West's smile faded. His gaze heated her skin and parted her lips. A set of chills coursed over her, rousing a blush on her cheeks. "Like I do."

Her toes curled inside her sneakers. She looked at him like that, too.

WEST SLID INTO Mary's room on Tina's shadow. He waited while the ladies hugged, then pulled up a chair and reintroduced himself.

"I remember," Mary said. She latched her drifting gaze onto West's damaged sleeve. "What happened to you?"

"Flesh wound." He smiled. He and his brothers had

used the phrase all their lives. Those two little words had stopped their mom from worrying and their dad from digging too deeply into whatever shenanigans they'd been into when the injury occurred. It was a wonder they weren't all as good with a bandage as Cole. They'd all taken their share of licks on ill-fated Garrett boy adventures. "Have you had any other visitors since we left?" he asked Mary.

"No. None. Why?"

Tina set a hand on her friend's arm. "We're just checking in."

West had seen her encourage and uplift lots of people when they were young. It was a trait he appreciated even more today. When he'd told her he blamed himself for letting Carl get away, Tina hadn't agreed, but she'd let him say it anyway. She'd let him put it out there without chastising him for a moment of lost composure. It was nice to be real with her, no pressure to put on the Good Sheriff Show. She'd always taken him as exactly who he was. Junk parts and all.

He rolled his shoulders in search of a comfortable position for his aching arm. "Have you thought of anything else?" he asked.

Tina's attention snapped to him. "I was going to ask her that."

He smiled. "Then ask."

Mary pressed her lips into a thin white line. "I've been mentally replaying the attack and those moments when he was in my home. Something that keeps going around in my scrambled thoughts is how he seemed so confident and casual about the whole affair. If not for the stutter, I'd have thought he was perfectly at ease breaking into my house and stealing a child. Who does that?"

"A very troubled man," Tina said.

West shifted in the chair and winced. Between his bruised ribs, knot on the head and a fresh gunshot wound, he was a mess. Thankfully, neither woman seemed to notice. "We think he's been planning this for a while. Was there anything else? Additional physical description. Clothing. Scent. Anything like that?"

Deep creases ran over Mary's brow. She chewed her lip for a long moment before answering. "I've seen the news. Saw the reports. The photos of Carl Morgan." She wet her lips and shifted her gaze from West to Tina. "I think I recognize him." Her voice was barely audible, even in the silent room. "I've seen him in your neighborhood and at the park where I take Lily for stroller rides."

That, too, fit perfectly with the scenario they'd developed. Carl had been plotting his actions. Choosing when and where to strike. West could only hope that he'd become overconfident and would make a mistake soon.

"Sometimes he was with another guy," Mary said. "The other one has red bushy hair and a beard. He wore old band T-shirts and looked like someone out of the 1960s."

Tina gasped. "Did he wear glasses? Round wire rims?"

"Yes."

West felt his blood pressure rising, heating his muscles and pounding in his head. "You know him?"

She lifted her hand from Mary's and set it on his chair. "I think she's describing Tucker."

The other patient who'd been suspiciously absent from her group on the day of the shooting.

West dialed Dispatch. His fingers curled tightly around the phone, thinking again of all the ways he'd like to make someone pay for this stress and heart-break. Tina didn't deserve any of this, and neither did that poor sweet baby. "Tell me you still have Tucker Bixby in detainment."

"Um." The deputy fielding calls at the station hesi-tated. The telltale sounds of a keyboard clicked in the quiet background.

Maybe the stars had aligned to deal them a good hand for once today.

The keyboarding sounds ended. "No, sir," Dis-patch reported. "He sobered up and Deputy Neely drove him home a little while ago."

"Get someone to his place. Right now. Pick him up and hold him there until I arrive." West discon-nected and sent texts with the new information to his team and Blake's. They'd hear it from Dispatch, but he wanted to be sure they knew it came from him and he wanted to be kept apprised.

He pushed onto his feet, feeling stronger by the minute. "I'm sorry to run, Mary, but we've got to go. You've been very helpful."

Together, he and Tina fled the hospital. She drove like a NASCAR driver all the way to Tucker Bixby's place and jammed it into Park beside a deputy's cruiser.

The home was small and yellow. A bungalow with a hibachi grill on the front porch and two camping chairs leaned against the railing. It wasn't much to look at, and a few years late on a much-needed coat of paint.

The front door opened, and Deputy Neely poked his head out. He cast a weary gaze at West and Tina, then motioned them inside. "This way." He led them through the silent home to the kitchen, then lowered to the floor beside a motionless Tucker.

Tina gasped. "Is he dead?"

"No." The deputy's Adam's apple bobbed slowly. "We released him not too long ago. He'd sobered up, and I brought him home. He was drunk when I found him at the park. Maybe high. He had a tent all set up. Said he wanted to be alone." Deputy Neely rechecked Tucker's vitals as he spoke. "When I drove him home he said he didn't want to be here. I didn't ask why. What if he was trying to tell me something? You know. Like a cry for help."

West circled the room, taking inventory of the scene. "And now?"

The deputy turned his attention toward the budding sound of a distant ambulance cry. "He's nonresponsive. Breaths are shallow. Pulse is slow and thin but there." He rubbed his forehead. "Possible overdose. Suicide attempt. I'm not sure. I checked his vitals, got him on his side and called 911."

Tina's knees buckled. She slid onto the floor with

a thud. Mouth open. Eyes heavy with tears. "I don't understand. He's been doing so well. Making so much progress. He hasn't struggled with drugs in a long while, and he told the group that his drinking was under control. He was proud of his positive strides. He was changing his life. Why would he do this?"

West wasn't sure if she meant the overdose, the potential involvement in Carl's scheme or both. As for the overdose, West wasn't convinced it was intentional. It'd been a long couple of days, especially for someone already suffering from anxiety and instability. "I'd like a look around."

The deputy stepped away. "There are bottles and paraphernalia on the table. Nothing at first glance to determine the time of the OD. I got here about four minutes ahead of you. Door was open. I didn't touch anything except him, looking for vitals. I called the ambulance a minute later when I found him."

West dashed the toe of his boot against the floor. "Door was open when you got here. Why?"

The deputy raised his brows.

West swore. "Carl had something to do with this." He lifted his eyes to the deputy. "Radio Dispatch. Get people out here looking for evidence of foul play and some way to prove Carl Morgan was here. If Tucker was part of Carl's plan and he went rogue, tried to run off or back out, then I'm willing to bet Carl would've had an opinion about it."

The ambulance pulled onto the curb with one final cry.

West led Tina back to his cruiser and helped her

inside. "I'm going to take a look around the house, talk to the EMTs and wait for the crime scene folks."

Then, he and Tina could head back to his place where he could take some more aspirin and wait for prelims and toxicology on Tucker.

Tina sat limply in the passenger seat and palmed his keys. "I think it's your turn to drive."

He accepted the offer. "I'm sorry this is happening to another member of your group."

She blinked a tear loose.

The near-death of Carl's possible partner in crime was far too convenient to be anything other than attempted murder.

Chapter Fifteen

Tina stripped out of her clothes inside West's bathroom, her body running more on autopilot than intention. Steam hovered over the surface of her bath like an apparition, as if the ghosts of her day had gathered in one spot to torture her. She sunk deep into the water until only her face remained dry. Her thoughts returned to Tucker. Had he been involved in the things that had happened to her? Had he wanted to die and failed? How long had he been using again, and how had she missed the signs?

Tina closed her eyes. Slipped completely beneath the surface. And the world went silent. She counted slowly to ten, releasing small bubbles of air, and reorganizing her thoughts before reemerging. Sadly, she couldn't live underwater, so she'd have to figure out her problems on land. She filled her lungs with oxygen, then coiled wet hair into a knot on top of her head.

She needed to talk to Tucker as soon as he woke up. There were so many questions to be asked. Most important, did he know where Lily was?

She rested her back against the smooth white surface of West's tub and prayed Tucker wouldn't die. For his sake and for hers.

She couldn't help wondering what else would go wrong. How much worse would things get before they got better? She kept thinking the worst had come, then something else would happen. A patient would overdose. The man she loved would be shot. Her heart ached at the thought. She loved West. Had denied it for years, but the reality of that love was too much to ignore, and she was tired of walking away from the thing she wanted most for herself. *Him.*

Thankfully, the sun had set, and this wretched day was coming to an end. West needed to rest. He played a good game, but she could see the pain in his eyes, in the way he moved a little slower now, and when his brows crowded sharply together at the slightest jostle of his injured arm. Why did he try to hide it from her? What was the point? She could always see through him, even before she'd pursued a career in human behavior. She didn't need a degree to know he was a terrible liar.

She'd have to deal with him later. Until then, the plan was to let the water wrinkle her skin and unknot her muscles. She skimmed her arms over the water's steamy surface and let her legs tip against the tub's side.

A set of quick knocks rattled the bathroom door. "Tina?" West asked.

She forced her eyes open. *Unbelievable.* "What happened now?"

She hated the unintentional bite in her voice. It wasn't his fault she was so tense, but surely he could see she was barely holding herself together. She needed this break. A moment to relieve the tension.

"Everything's fine," he called back.

"Then why are you knocking?" She hoisted herself from the water. That didn't make any sense. "Never mind. I'm coming. Just a minute." Tina wrapped a giant towel around her heated skin and padded quickly across the room. She opened the door with one hand and supported her towel with the other. "Are you sick?" She looked at his bandaged arm. The blood hadn't come through since he'd last changed the gauze.

His eyes met hers with a look of shock. "I didn't mean to interrupt," he rushed. "I just know how the last couple days have gone for us, and I figured we should talk before something else went wrong. I'm making coffee and maybe some food if you think you can eat. When you're finished."

"We should talk?" Tina didn't like the sound of that. In her experience, arranged talks usually ended in bad news, hurt feelings or a fight. The exact opposite of how she'd wanted to spend whatever quiet time the day would give them. "Let me get dressed."

West seemed to notice then that he'd literally pulled her out of the bath for this. His gaze dropped from her eyes to her exposed shoulders, then skimmed her neck and collarbone, where drops of water were beginning to cool her flushed skin. He didn't stop there. He continued to take her in, head to toe, without apology, and she widened the door several inches to give him a better view. *Too bad he was so determined to be a gentleman.*

His eyes returned to hers with an expression she'd seen on him many times before. The look was heated, raw and sexy as hell. Desire painted his skin and tensed his frame. He was clearly struggling not to reach for her, when all she wanted in that moment was to be touched by him.

"West." He'd rejected her advances last night, but he hadn't looked at her like this in years. She pushed the door open wide. Cool air rushed into the room, tightening her skin into gooseflesh and drawing her closer to the heat of him. Surely he felt it, too. Whatever this thing was that crackled and burned in the air between them. It wasn't just attraction. Not just chemistry. She'd had those things before. This was different. Palpable. Indescribable. Powerful. If this was all in her head, then she was in serious trouble because it felt 100 percent real to her. Like she and West had never truly been apart, as if their bond had never been broken, only stretched by distance and the hands of time.

And it was snapping back with bone-jarring intensity.

She set a hand on his chest and marveled at the pounding of his heart beneath her fingertips. He felt it, too.

Confliction pursed his lips and lined his brow as she traced a slow path over his shoulder, enjoying the feel of chiseled muscle beneath her fingers, watching closely for signs she'd gone too far.

Desire darkened West's eyes. He dropped his head forward, pressing his forehead to hers and wrapping her in the strength of his body, as if he thought she might disappear.

She inhaled the scent of his cologne, intoxicated by the moment. West was everywhere. His hands on her skin. His heart next to hers. She tipped her head back, savoring the moment she'd waited so long for. "Tell me this is real," she whispered breathlessly.

"This," he whispered back, tugging her closer and gripping her tight, "this is everything." His voice was velvet on her aching heart, and his hold arched her back sensually.

The towel lost its grip, but didn't fall. Much like Tina, it was captured in the moment, held tight by the press of their bodies.

She moved her gaze to his lips, longing to feel them on her, to watch them trace paths over her skin and pull moans from her core. "Kiss me." She stared into his stormy eyes. "I don't need a protector right now," she whispered. "I don't need a gentleman or a sheriff. I need you."

West pulled back an inch, emotion warring in his eyes.

"Please." The anticipation of rejection scorched her cheeks and knotted in her stomach. Was this really where she was now? Begging for physical comforts from a man she'd never stopped loving, one who couldn't even decide if he wanted to kiss her?

She dropped her chin and slid her arms away from his neck. Better to catch the towel before it fell completely and she died naked of humiliation.

West wrapped strong fingers around her wrists and returned them to his shoulders. Her towel loosened further, but his hot blue eyes never left hers. "You're sure about this?"

"Yes."

He lowered his mouth to hers, vanquishing the fear of rejection on impact. His kiss warmed her soul. It filled her with nostalgia for what they had and new hope for what they could become, if he still wanted her when the nightmares were over.

He broke the kiss far too soon with a growl and a pant. Tina's towel fell, and she was glad to be rid of it. There was no time to watch him toil over whether or not this was the right thing to do. She needed him. Now. She shoved his T-shirt upward, away from her. Over his head. The moment it hit the floor, his hands were back on her body, lifting her off the ground and onto the countertop. Her legs wrapped his waist on instinct and locked against his back. The new position pressed her fully against the length of him. She curled her fingers in his hair and dissolved into the effects of his divine and practiced attention.

Finally, in the moment she needed it most, West devoured her in hungry head-to-toe kisses until there was nothing left for her to do but fall apart in his hands.

WEST CREPT OUT of the bedroom where he'd held Tina until she was soundly asleep. Making love to her had been the last thing on his mind when he'd knocked on the bathroom door. He'd only been thinking of losing her again. He'd wanted to let her know that he had something to tell her, and that they should talk before they were interrupted by a new catastrophe.

He shuffled to the kitchen and poured a glass of ice water. He rolled it against his forehead before gulping it down. That woman made it impossible to keep his hands off her. His will was strong enough to survive three brothers, a war and every criminal in the county, but she looked at him sideways, and he was putty. Never mind when she *asked* for something. As if he could tell her no. As if resistance was possible. It had nearly killed him to step away the last time she'd confronted him with her desire. At least then she'd had her clothes on.

He poured another glass and tried to remember he was only human. Sure, he'd promised her he'd behave like a professional until Carl was caught and her life was right-side up again, but she'd said please. *Please.* He finished the second glass of water and set the empty cup in the sink. He leaned over the counter, bracing his hands and hanging his head in shame.

Deeply satisfied shame.

She was going to be doubly pissed when he told her what he'd been trying to tell her. It was his fault her mom was in the wind.

"Everything okay?" Tina stood in the hallway wearing nothing but his T-shirt. Her hands curled around the corner of the kitchen wall as if she wasn't sure she should come in.

West tried not to stare at the way his shirt slid off her shoulder, revealing the creamy expanse of skin along her collarbone and dusting the ivory flesh of her thighs with its hem. "I thought you were sleeping."

"I was until you left. Did something happen?"

"No. I'm going to make some coffee, review the files on Carl and see if I can think of something we missed. Can I pour you a mug?"

Tina shook her head. "Just water for me. I'm hoping to fall back asleep soon." She dragged a palm across his bare abdomen on her way to the cupboard for a glass.

His muscles tightened with recent memories of similar caresses. "We have to talk," he blurted. Not exactly how he wanted the unfortunate conversation to begin, but if he didn't tell her soon, and she touched him like that again, they'd be back in bed and he'd be in deeper trouble.

Tina froze. The cup stopped inches from her bee-stung lips, still pink and full from the tug of his teeth and brush of his stubble. A playful smile curved her cheeks. "Are you breaking up with me?"

He took the cup from her and set it aside. "This is serious."

Her mouth pulled down at the corners. "Please don't look so guilty. I know you think you took advantage of me, but you didn't. I'm a big girl, and I asked for it."

The gleam in her eye nearly derailed his concentration. "It's not that." He scrubbed a hand over his face. "I didn't mean for that to happen."

Her eyes went soft and round. Her hands traced the curves of her sides with uncertainty. "I know I'm different now. Older, but I thought I did okay in there." A bashful smile lifted her cheek.

"Stop." Images of all Tina's new curves sprang back to mind. That little smile didn't help, either. "You've got to stop talking to me about your body, or I'm putting you over my shoulder, and we're going back to bed. Then I'll never get to say what I'm trying to say."

She gave his shoulder a long look. "Okay. What's this about?"

"Your dad. You know what? Maybe we should sit down." West led her to the couch and started at the beginning. He laid it all bare from the arrest to the hearing. "I pushed for the maximum sentence. I did it because I blamed him for you leaving. I blamed him for hurting you. I knew you hated him, but I hadn't understood until then." He swallowed a brick of anger wedging in his throat. Could feel his temper slipping at the memory of what that monster had put Tina through. "I knew things were bad at your house, but I had no idea until I read his file. Once I knew, I made sure his charges stuck. I volunteered as a character witness. I personally delivered the files to the prosecutor and pretty well offered your father up on a silver platter to be sure he got the worst he could get." West gave her his most pleading look and prayed for the right words to make her understand. "I thought I was doing the right thing. I finally understood why you'd wanted to leave so badly, and even if it was years too late and you were already gone, I wanted to protect you like I should have all along."

Tina blinked, but didn't speak. She relaxed against the couch.

"I've felt awful ever since," West said. "He was on trial for the bar fight, but my help had made it more like he was being charged with dozens of crimes all at once. His history of violence left the jury beyond words. They gave him the maximum sentence for what he did to that guy at the bar. The victory I felt disappeared once he was led away. That wasn't how our courts should work. Your dad's trial was unfair because his own sheriff had a finger on the scales. I think that's why I didn't visit your mom." He dared another look in her direction.

Tina looked as if he'd slapped her.

"Say something." *Yell. Scream. Anything.* He deserved it, and he could take it.

"You let me confess my deepest family secrets to you yesterday, and you already knew? You'd read his file with all our bloody details. Literally. And you let me go on. Do you know how hard that was for me? I've never told anyone about the things I went through."

West rolled her complaint around a few times. "You're not mad because I had a hand in your dad's extensive sentence or your mom's flight? You're mad I didn't interrupt you yesterday and blurt out that I already knew the things you were telling me?"

She crossed her arms.

"I wanted to hear them from you. I want to hear

everything you have to say. If this is going to work—" he motioned from his chest to hers "—then you're going to have to keep talking, Tina. You have to let me in, all the time, not just when you've had a decade to think it over."

"Me?" She poked her chest. "Me! What about you? You just finished confessing a secret of your own. Why? Is it because we had sex?"

His jaw dropped. Was she out of her ever-loving mind? "You think I'm trying to pay you off with secrets for sex?" Maybe her dad had messed her up more deeply than he'd realized. "I don't want anything from you."

Tina's cheeks went white. Her arms dropped limply to her sides.

He recognized the misunderstanding at once and closed the distance between them. He wrapped her in his arms, despite a mild protest on her part before she returned his embrace with fervor and tears. "I'm sorry I didn't tell you sooner. I knew you were back in town the minute you got here, and that's when I should've come to you with the truth. I told myself I was respecting your boundaries by not showing up on your doorstep. You were the one who'd left, and you didn't look me up when you came back. I assumed you didn't want to see me, and I let that be my excuse for not knocking on your door." He cupped her face in his hands and stared into her distrusting eyes. "Please don't let what happened between us today confuse you. That was done out of love."

She looped her arms around his neck and buried her face into the curve of his neck.

"Come on." He kept her tight against his side as he led her back to his room.

She climbed into bed and rolled away without a word.

The steady throb of pain from his gunshot wound was nothing compared to the iron fist squeezing his heart. West hit the lights on his way out, reminding himself to breathe. He'd just gotten her back, and he wasn't ready to lose her again.

He never would be.

Chapter Sixteen

West jogged through the house toward his ringing phone and snatched it off the kitchen countertop. Blake's face lit the screen. It had been hours since West had received any new leads, and West was beginning to feel the grip of fear in his gut. "Tell me you've got good news," West said. His muscles tensed in anticipation of the answer. They'd had a lot of news these past two days, but none of it had been good, and West needed a break, or at least a viable lead to keep his mind off the angry woman in his bed.

"I'm not sure if it's good news," Blake answered, "but I'm at the hospital with the OD victim, and he's awake."

"He lived?" Maybe West's luck was starting to turn around after all. Tucker's pulse was barely existent when the EMTs loaded him into the ambulance. "Is he coherent? Talking?"

"He's something," Blake said.

"Well, what's that supposed to mean?" West ground his teeth. "Did he make a statement or not?"

"He's not talking."

West lifted a hand in exasperation. "Then make him talk."

"Can't. I showed him my badge, and he demanded I arrest Carl Morgan for trying to kill him. When I asked about his own role in the shootings and kidnapping, he shut down and asked for a lawyer."

"Of course." West had never met a criminal who wouldn't drop their demands in a heartbeat to cover their own ass. "Try getting the information another way. Refocus on Carl as a killer. We can arrest Tucker later. Right now we just need to know where that baby is."

"No can do," Blake said. "He's refusing to speak without the lawyer, and for the record, I tried to make him talk, but he pushed the little help button at his bedside and told the nurse I was harassing him. I got kicked out by a woman in scrubs with little bears on them."

"Try again."

"She's guarding his door. There's nothing I can do now but wait. The federal public defender will be here first thing in the morning."

West swore. So much for administering the Garrett charm. He rolled his head between his shoulders. Blake had always been a bit of a battering ram, but he normally got things done that way. Cole was the sweet talker, but West suspected calling him in wouldn't make a difference on Tucker. That guy was done talking to law enforcement tonight. "Maybe Cole can distract the nurse and you can get another shot at our accomplice."

Tina crept into view. She'd traded his T-shirt for soft cotton pants and a sweater. She'd been in West's room for several hours. Had she not been able to sleep, or had the phone woken her? "Let me talk to him."

West pulled the phone from his ear. "Blake?"

"Tucker," she corrected, apparently having eavesdropped on the conversation. "He'll talk to me. I know him, and being involved in this must be killing him. It's not who he is. He's sensitive and overthinking. He's not a bully. Far from it."

West pressed the phone back to his ear. "Did you hear that?"

"Yeah. Get her over here," Blake said.

West disconnected and pocketed the phone. He stepped closer to Tina, longing to pull her back into his arms.

She stepped away with a deep frown, as if she could read his mind. "You should get dressed. I'll grab my coat and shoes."

TINA WAS OFFICIALLY sick of this hospital and a growing number of other things. Like people who kept big secrets, for example, herself included. Keeping secrets was a terrible decision, destined to end in tragedy. No one ever kept happy things to themselves. They only swallowed the dark, damaging things, and those bitter truths had a way of coming back up eventually. From now on, she was only interested in the immediate truth.

Blake was easy to spot in the long white hallway, a tall, dark presence in an otherwise blinding wing.

He spoke softly with an old woman in teddy bear scrubs who didn't appear to be taking any of his orders. The hospital was her turf. Just like West had told her before they visited Mary. Blake's badge would only do so much good here. The low tenor of his voice ricocheted off the bare walls in waves of murmured agitation. Tina couldn't make out the words, but his brow was pinched. His posture was stiff, and his hands moved fast enough between them to set him into flight.

"She won't let him back in the room," West interpreted, keeping pace at her side. "Tucker says Blake's upsetting him."

Blake took notice of their approach and turned to face them.

The nurse blocked the threshold to room three fifteen. "Evening, Sheriff." She nodded at West before turning to Tina. "Miss."

"This is Tina Ellet," West explained. "She's your patient's therapist. She insisted on seeing him when she heard the news."

The woman gave Tina a hard look. "What sort of therapist?"

Tina pulled a business card from the pocket of her coat and handed it to the woman. "I'm a licensed clinical psychologist specializing in trauma recovery."

The nurse pocketed Tina's card. "He's had a trauma, but that's new. How can he already be your patient?"

Tina's client list was confidential, but she still needed to see Tucker. "I'm also a concerned friend," she said, trying to sound cordial instead of angry. "I came as soon as I heard he was here." None of the things happening to her were the nurse's fault. It wasn't fair to take them out on her.

The nurse didn't look convinced.

"You can come inside with me," Tina suggested. "See for yourself if he wants me to leave." She crossed her fingers that Tucker wouldn't be too much of a coward to face her after his involvement in her hellish nightmare. She was certain his gentle nature would make him bubble over with guilt and shame at the sight of her. If he didn't send her away, he'd talk, but there was a good chance those same characteristics would make him want to hide. In which case, she'd be booted back into the hall with the Garretts. Not a place she wanted to be at the moment.

Her heart was still stewing from West's confession. He'd known about her childhood traumas for more than a year. Residual humiliation burned her cheeks. It had nearly killed her to finally voice those very painful, private memories, and he'd sat there, letting her ramble on like an idiot, confessing things he'd already known. It was an unexpected blow to her pride after what had happened between them physically. Though, in his defense, he had come to tell her they needed to talk before she begged him to take her. Her head fell slightly forward, and she pressed hot fingertips to her forehead.

The nurse huffed. "I can see you're truly troubled. Not like the agent over there." She pushed the door open and gave it a gentle knock. "Tucker? There's a friend here to see you."

"Who?" Tucker's voice was surprisingly sharp.

Tina pushed her way into the room. "Me."

Tucker's eyes went wide. "Ms. Ellet. What are you doing here?" His reddish hair was mussed and tucked behind both ears. His beard was ragged and unkempt. He sounded well, but he looked every bit the part of a man who'd recently been near death.

She tried not to bite her tongue completely off. "I came to check on you. I heard what happened, and I was really worried." The sugary sweetness of her voice rang false and fairly malicious in her ears.

"You were?" He flicked his gaze from Tina to the nurse and back. "I didn't do that heroin," he said. "I took some pills and blacked out, but I shouldn't have done that."

Tina took a tentative stop forward. "I'm just glad you're okay now."

"You are?" Disbelief colored his tone.

"Yes." She was also glad to see he was clear of thought. That would help her tremendously as soon as she ditched the nurse. "You look really good, too. I expected you to be asleep after everything you've been through."

The nurse took a step toward the hallway, letting the door swing with her. "If everything's okay, I guess I'll let you two visit."

"Yeah. Thank you." Tucker nodded. He straightened in the bed, adjusting his pillows and arranging the puddled blankets more smoothly over his legs. "Come on in. There's a chair. Do you want water?"

"No." Tina lowered herself into the bedside armchair, concentrating on her breathing and composure. A piece of her worried about Tucker. She'd guided and counseled him for nearly a year. How long had he been using drugs? How much of that time had he spent with Carl? How long had he known about Carl's plans?

"Are you okay?" Tucker asked.

She raised her eyes to him. "No. I'm not. Someone took my baby."

His mouth opened. He shut it without a sound.

"You missed our last session. Did you know that Steven is dead now? That someone shot him in the parking lot? He was right beside me. It was terrifying."

Tucker's cheeks darkened, and he looked away. "I heard about that. I'm sorry."

"Thank you. I'd thought it was the worst thing I would ever experience, but then I learned someone has been stalking me, breaking into my home, watching my baby and me." Images of her late husband's face washed into mind beside fresh memories of West being shot. Had Carl done the same thing to Thomas? Hidden in the woods to end his life with the curl of one finger?

"I didn't know that he'd—" Tucker clamped his lips tight. "I'm sorry."

"Didn't know what?" she asked, training her gaze on his. Tina tried to make herself seem smaller and less threatening. The guise should've been easy given her circumstances, but at the moment she struggled not to tell him exactly what she thought of a grown man playing the "innocent" card. He might not want to admit it, but he'd known something was monstrously wrong, and he'd done nothing to stop it. At the very least, Tucker was complacent, but he was not innocent. "What didn't you know?" she pressed. "Is it something about my daughter? If it is, then you have to tell me." She leaned toward him and gripped the safety railing along his bed. Traitorous tears blurred her vision. "I don't care about anything else. I just need to get my baby back."

Tucker looked at the door behind her. "I don't want to go to jail."

Tina nearly choked on her disgust. "Would you really let an infant die because you want to protect yourself? Is that who you are? Who you want to be?" She shoved off her chair hard enough to send it scraping loudly across the floor.

The door swung open and West barged inside. He moved between Tina and Tucker, evaluating the situation before turning to her with an expectant look.

She reached for him, and he locked his protective arms around her.

"My baby is out there somewhere," she told Tucker. "She's scared. She could be hurt. Maybe worse. And you're in here, all tucked into your little hospital bed, being guarded by a nurse from the big bad lawmen." Her voice climbed in decibels with every new word. "What is wrong with you?" She pushed away from

West and fell back onto her chair, wiping frantically at the falling tears. "I'm so sorry." She batted blurred eyes at Tucker. "I didn't mean to yell."

Tucker leaned away as if she'd slapped him.

She'd probably ruined everything by screaming at him. Wasn't that exactly the kind of behavior she and Tucker had both grown up fearing?

The door opened once more, and the nurse arrived with a scowl. "Out."

"Wait," Tucker said.

Tina held her breath. She said a prayer.

"It's okay. I want to talk to these two."

Air whooshed from her burning lungs when the nurse retreated, closing the door behind her.

Tucker tugged his ratty beard and fixed his gaze on Tina. "Carl talked about a lot of crazy stuff, but he never did any of it. I told myself he was just nuts."

"What?" West stormed Tucker's bedside. "You didn't think to report it? Not even to Tina, if not to the sheriff's department?"

"No."

West gripped the back of his neck and took a lap around the room, presumably to keep himself from giving Tucker another reason to be in the hospital.

Tina shook her head in disbelief. "He talked with you about murder and kidnapping. You should have told someone. Told me. I could've stopped him. None of this had to happen."

"What else does he have planned?" West asked, stopping at Tina's side. "And where did he take the baby?"

"I don't know." Tucker released his beard. A look of resolution narrowed his eyes. "I was with Carl last year when your husband died."

Tina gasped. "What?" She forced herself to breathe. To make sense of the admission. "What do you mean?" she asked. Her stomach lurching at the implication.

"Off the record?" he asked West.

"Hell no." West's hand found Tina's, and he squeezed.

Tucker dipped his chin in a stiff acceptance. "Carl showed up at my place that night with a case of beer, wanting to go camping. He didn't have any gear, and he knew from group that I'm an outdoorsman. At first I said no, but after a few drinks, I agreed to go. He drove my truck so I wouldn't get pulled over. I set up the tent where he wanted, built the fire. Had a few more beers, then I passed out. Carl woke me the next day. He'd packed up the truck, and he was in a big hurry to go home. He said his mom's living facility called. She'd fallen, and we needed to go. I slept on the ride home. I didn't think anything of it until word got around about your husband. I remembered all the things Carl had said about him, and when I asked where we went camping, he got angry. He said we could never tell anyone we were camping that night or they'd link us to you and accuse us of murder. He said the sheriff wouldn't care if it was true—he'd just want to close the case and punish someone for a man's death. Our histories of instability, and my problems with substance abuse, made us the perfect scapegoats."

"You bought that?" West snapped.

"Yeah. I mean, you hear that stuff all the time on the news."

West's body went rigid. "You had to know it was Carl who shot him."

"I didn't. I was out cold until he woke me to go home. I still can't remember exactly where we camped, and he never told me. It wasn't as if we were at an official campground. We just pulled off somewhere, walked a bit and set up for the night. He seemed to know where we were going, so I went with it. All I knew was that his sudden desire to camp on the night of your husband's death was a heavy coincidence."

Tina was officially numb.

West released her hand to cradle his injured arm against his chest a moment before crossing the free arm over it. "We've got ballistics out on that case now. If it was the same gun, we'll know. For the record, Carl was wrong about me arresting anyone just to close the case, but I'll damn sure charge him with murder if those results come back as a match, and you're going down as an accessory."

Tucker frowned. "When do I get my lawyer?"

"Public defender will be here in the morning. You can wait for representation, or you can start putting someone else first for once and help me save this baby's life. You have to know something we can use to find her."

Tucker seemed to weigh West's words. "I don't know where they are. Carl and I aren't friends like that. We drink together sometimes. Usually when he arranges it. He's obsessed with Tina. Has been since I met him in group, but he was following her before that. She bought him a coffee, or something, and he couldn't get over it. He said he asked about her at the drive-through window when the cashier told him his order was paid for. He was so happy, he followed her home that day. He's never stopped. After her husband died, I tried to put some distance between us, but he was insistent. He kept me close. I could tell he was watching me in case I decided to talk. Then, one night we went to play pool. He drove. When we left, he couldn't find his keys, so we walked to his house, but without his keys we couldn't get in. I picked the lock on the back door for him." Tucker's face turned red. "We'd talked about that a few days before. I learned it growing up. My dad would lock me in the basement." He shook his head hard, as if he could somehow erase the memory. "The door opened, but he didn't invite me inside. I had to walk home alone from there. I woke up on my lawn. A few weeks later, I picked him up to go fishing, but the address he gave me was a trailer."

"Not the house you broke into," West finished.

"No," Tucker said. "The farmhouse wasn't his. He'd tricked me into breaking into it."

Tina forced another round of vomit back down her throat. Was she sleeping while two drunks had broken in? What had Carl done while he was inside?

Tucker turned tired eyes on her. "That was your house, wasn't it?"

She nodded. "What about my dog? Did he bark or growl?"

"No dog."

Tina's mind scrambled back, thankful that Ducky wasn't there. That meant that Lily wasn't born yet, either. "I lost my keys last spring," she said. "I was struggling with Thomas's death and the pregnancy. I forgot things. Slept all the time. I bet Carl took them when he came in." Then he could let himself in anytime he wanted, as if her home was his home, too.

"Why didn't you report the break-in when you realized it was Tina's house?" West asked.

Tucker made an ugly noise. "He had me, man. On both counts. I was drunk and doing stuff I wasn't supposed to. I'd have wound up in jail right beside him."

Tina smacked her palms against the arms of the uncomfortable chair. "What do you think is going to happen now? All you've done is put off the inevitable. You could've at least saved Steven's life and spared my baby by doing the right thing a long time ago."

Tucker flopped against his pillow. "I wish I could help you find your baby. I've tried to think of where he might be, but Carl never gives all the facts. He talks in circles. Never completes a story. He just gives enough detail to drag you in and shove you under."

"Think," West growled. "Give it your best try. We're running blind out there."

"All I know is that he's obsessed with Tina. Her home, baby, dog, everything. He thinks she's the perfect mother, and he really hates his."

Tucker's deflated expression broke Tina's heart. He'd trusted the wrong person. Let substance abuse cloud his judgment. "You told Agent Garrett that Carl tried to kill you. Is that true?"

"Yeah. I don't do heroin."

West scoffed. "Are you saying Carl forcefully injected you with the drug? And you couldn't stop him?"

"I'm saying I was stoned. Out cold on oxy and I woke up in here. They pumped my stomach, dosed me up with Narcan and told me I tried to kill myself. I don't do needles." A shiver wiggled down his frame.

The door swung open and Cole blew inside. "West." The look of excitement on his face snapped Tina back to life.

"What'd you get?" West asked.

"I just spoke with the man who owns the property where Carl's trailer sits." A wide smile pulled over his lips. "He said Carl called him yesterday and asked to use his cabin near the lake for a few nights. The man agreed."

Tina popped onto her feet. "You know where they are?"

Cole nodded. "I think we do."

West wrapped a strong hand around her wrist and led her toward the door. "Hang tight, Tucker. There'll be a deputy outside your door standing guard with the nurse. Don't get any ideas about leaving early."

"Good luck," Tucker said. "I really do hope you find him."

Cole followed West and Tina into the hallway, where Blake joined their ranks.

They filled Blake in as they hurried to the waiting elevator. The exact words were lost to Tina, whose ears were ringing loudly with hope.

They finally knew where her baby was.

Chapter Seventeen

The sheriff's department buzzed with activity. Men and women in various uniforms poured in and out of the door like bees to a hive. They spoke hurriedly into walkie-talkies and cell phones, ramping up Tina's already sprinting pulse.

This could really be it. The moment she got her hands on Lily again. This time she might never let her go.

West caught the door and held it as the next group of officials spilled into the night. "Ladies first."

Tina passed into the busy department, squinting against the harsh glow of fluorescent lights. Her heart thundered against her ribs, aching to burst from exertion or just break free.

"Look who beat us here," West said. "Mom, you remember Tina."

A familiar face broke free from the crowd. "Of course." Her sweet voice tugged at Tina's heartstrings. She pulled Tina against her chest with strong, motherly arms and gently stroked her hair. "Oh, how I've missed you."

Tina held her tight. She smelled exactly the same. A perfect blend of cookies and mountain air.

His mother pulled back for a thorough look at Tina. A bright smile graced her face. She'd gone gray since they'd last met, but that was no wonder surrounded by Garrett men and their thirst for danger.

Tina fought a wave of tears and nostalgia. Even after the way she'd left West, his mother looked as happy to see her as if she was a long-lost daughter of her own. She wasn't sure she'd be as understanding if someone hurt Lily.

"She and Dad are here to help," West said. "Dad will be working the desk, aiding Dispatch, should something unexpected arise. He knows the job as well as I do. He did it for twenty-five years. Mom's the moral support."

His mother extended an arm, finger pointed, and swept it in front of her, indicating the mass of busy officials. "I keep them in line."

Tina dragged her attention from the woman she'd often pretended was her mother and fixed it on West. "What do you mean by unexpected? Like what?"

The corner of West's mouth curled up. "We don't know. That's what makes it unexpected." He moved into Tina's personal space and planted a kiss on her head. "We've got this, and you don't need to worry. We're taking a trained team to scout the area and confirm Carl's presence. Once we've got that, we'll move in silently and follow Blake's lead on hostage extraction. Carl will never know we're there until Lily's safely away and we all move in."

Tina considered the possibility. A horde of men, trained or not, marching up to and entering a cabin with only one man and a baby inside. How could Carl *not* know they were there? The cabins along the lake were all old, weathered and creaky. Fairly dilapidated as well, if memory served. Those buildings were good for camping and shelter, but not exactly the kind of place a bunch of federal agents could descend upon silently. Then there was Lily. To think she wouldn't wail at the sight of a strange man in SWAT gear, or whatever they would be wearing, was naive at best. Though, dumb seemed more fitting.

"We've got this," West repeated. He pressed the pad of his thumb to the space between her brows and smoothed the deep frown that had gathered there.

"You keep saying that, but it doesn't make it true." She glanced at West's mom, suddenly self-conscious at the way he freely touched her in public. Did everyone know what had happened between them? If they didn't before, they must now. Heat rose into her cheeks, and she forced her thoughts back to what mattered most. Lily. "What if this is all a ruse? He could have set the whole thing up just to lead you into danger. He could have the cabin booby-trapped. What if he's really staying at the owner's home, holding him hostage? He might have forced him to make that suspiciously helpful and conveniently timed call to Cole."

West hung his head and peeked up at her through thick dark lashes, a look of humor and humility on his face. "You know, your lack of faith in us is a little insulting."

His mom rubbed his back and grinned. "You can take it. Chin up. I'm going to go check on your father." She winked in Tina's direction and was gone.

Tina stepped back, out of West's reach. "It's not that I don't think you can do what you say you can do. It's that this isn't the first time you thought you had him, and the last time you followed a lead on Carl, you were shot. Then Tucker was nearly killed. And that was just today."

"I'm going to be fine."

She shook her head. "It's more than that. I don't know if I can handle another crushing blow. Every time I think I'll get Lily back—" she pressed her hands against the aching void in her chest "—something goes very wrong, and that hope is torn away."

West's expression turned sober. He moved in closer and dragged her back to him. "C'mere." He lowered his cheek until it lined with hers. His breath washed over her ear. "No one else is getting hurt. Not Lily. Not me. Maybe Carl." She felt his cheek pull into a smile against hers.

West was clearly in his element, on some kind of adrenaline high, like athletes before a big game. His broad palms found the deep curves of her waist. "My deputies are already patrolling. Deputy Neely is positioned on the main road closest to the cabin. The others have eyes on every route in and out, including anything passable by four-wheeler. If Carl's there, he won't get away." West pressed a kiss against her temple and straightened with a crooked smile. "Cole's out there with a drone for aerial surveillance. If all that hasn't put your mind at ease, let me show you something that will."

He pulled her in the direction of his parents. "Dad's staying right here until it's over." They stopped at the desk where Dispatch fielded calls. "He'll be able to hear our chatter, process all the information and make decisions as needed in the event my comms go out or I have to go radio silent."

His dad saluted as they approached. "It's nice to see you again, Tina. It hasn't been the same around here without you."

She forced a smile through quivering lips. "Thank you." West's dad had apparently kept all her family's dirty little secrets. As the former sheriff, he knew the Ellets well. Part of her had always wondered if he'd filled West in on just how damaged his girlfriend really was. Based on West's confession today, his father had never told. He'd hauled her dad home more times than she could count, drunk, angry or both, and he'd warned him never to lay a hand on her. The former sheriff had promised to rain hell on him if he ever saw a mark on Tina. The sad memory evoked a strange smile. West really was like his father, and both men were ones she wanted in hers and Lily's lives.

He patted the arm of the chair at his side. "I set you up a chair right here. This way if you hear anything you don't understand, I can translate."

"Thank you," she said, as much for the chair as for the hundred times he'd given her teenage heart hope for a better future. Tina folded her arms, but couldn't bring herself to sit. A stubborn bubble of optimism filled her chest. Logic told her not to get too excited. *Remember,* she warned herself, *you keep getting punched down.* And finding her footing again had been harder after every new hit.

West pressed a button on the spread of radio equipment before them. White noise and distant voices piped through the speaker. "If you sit here and listen, you'll know everything that's going on. You won't have to wait for us to come back to know what we found. It'll be like you're right there with us. Only here. Safe."

West and his dad traded pointed looks.

She didn't ask. Listening from a safe distance seemed a solid compromise to stealing a cruiser and trying to follow them unnoticed. If Lily was out there, Tina wanted to be there to comfort her frightened little heart. She could only hope that if things went exactly as West described, he would return for her and bring her immediately to see her daughter. Until then, the waiting would be unbearable. There were too many unknowns. Too many variables and what-ifs. More than that, there was too much at risk.

West wiggled the empty chair.

"Thanks." She forced her wooden legs to bend and fell onto the seat at his father's side.

Blake's head popped up from the huddle around a broad metal desk. "Sheriff."

West gave her a confident smile and went to join his brother.

"I've got eyes on the cabin." Cole's voice rang loud and clear through the speaker in front of her.

The room stilled. Conversations and movement instantly halted. They'd been waiting for this moment.

West was back at her side, pressing a button on the radio. "Do you see any movement down there?"

"Negative. It's too dark and ground cover is heavy."

"What about a vehicle?" West asked, casting his attention toward his father. "Do you see the red pickup truck?"

Silence beat in her ears. A chill of suspense beaded her skin into gooseflesh and stood the fine hairs along her arms and across the back of her neck at attention.

The crowd seemed to hold its breath in collective anticipation.

"Affirmative," Cole finally announced. "I have eyes on a late-model Ford pickup. License plate unreadable."

The mass of frozen officials burst into action.

"Good job, brother," West said, pushing and releasing the button once more. "Stand down for backup." A broad smile split his face as he leaned in to kiss Tina's lips. "I know you're still mad at me for not telling you I knew about your past."

She stiffened in his grasp. Half embarrassed to hear the words spoken in a crowded room.

He planted another quick kiss. "I won't let you down like that again, and I'm about to make you forget I screwed up at all." He pinned her with a sexy, heated kiss before turning away without a goodbye.

He stretched one arm overhead, circling his wrist. "Roll out."

Tina watched breathlessly as the room emptied

and the darkened lot beyond the windows was illuminated in headlights.

West's mom moved to the door, watching as her boys and their teams drove away. Her eyelids slipped shut for several moments before reopening with a look of pride that Tina had seen on her countless times before. When the last set of taillights had gone, she turned for the desk. "Now, we wait. Can I get you a distraction from the break room, sweetie? Some cold water or hot tea?"

"No, thank you." Tina pressed unsteady hands against her middle, attempting to crush the nerves and keep the last food she'd eaten in place.

A dozen quiet voices flooded the speaker, chattering to one another in some sort of code made of slang and foreign acronyms. West's dad tapped his fingers against the table and whistled, completely at ease.

A miserable thought presented itself then, coiling regret through Tina's heart. She hadn't said goodbye to West. If anything happened to him, if she lost him again, he'd never know how much he meant to her, or that she wasn't mad like he thought.

She understood why he did what he did to her father. If she thought it would have made a difference, she'd have testified, too, but no one asked. Maybe that was also part of West's doing. Either way, her dad had always breezed through his arrests. A night in jail here. A week there. Inevitably released due to overcrowding or some other nonsense. Then again, he'd always been a drunken menace, never a violent offender. That had surely made the difference this time, and West had done the right thing. She also wished she'd told him that he wasn't responsible for her mother's disappearance. Tina should've made him understand that instead of pulling away to stew about her own burned pride. It had been her mother's choice, and hers alone, to leave without so much as a phone call or forwarding address, and truth be told, her mother had left Tina a long time ago.

Her phone buzzed against her leg, and she flipped it over with haste. If it was West, then she'd respond with the words she wished she'd have said sooner. *I love you.*

Surprisingly, the text was from an unknown number. She swiped her thumb across the screen to read the note. Maybe West used another phone during an operation like this one.

The message was mixed media. A picture of Lily in her winter coat, strapped in a car seat, plus a line of text.

Side lot. Now. Or it's the last time you'll see your baby. Come alone. Tell no one.

She gasped, turning quickly to West's dad.

He raised his bushy brows. "Everything okay?"

She returned her eyes to the little screen. The time on the dashboard clock behind Lily read 10:10. The same time her phone had in the corner. The picture was taken now. In a car. Not at a cabin.

Now or never, Tina.

She stretched to her feet. "Fine," she answered West's dad belatedly.

He puckered his brow. "You sure?"

She nodded too quickly, feeling suddenly unsteady and flushed. "Yeah. I'm just going to— I changed my mind about the water." She bumbled away from the seat.

He narrowed sharp, knowing eyes. Twenty-five years as the sheriff had apparently given him an intuition about liars that Tina had failed to achieve. After all, if she'd seen Carl for who he was, none of this would be happening.

She pointed at the speaker, where voices continued to spout cop lingo and military jargon alongside map coordinates for a cabin that they would soon find empty. At least West was safe, barring any booby traps. "I'll be back before they get started." She turned for the hallway to the break room and rear exit. "I'll hurry."

She jogged away, looking repeatedly over her shoulder in case Mr. Garrett followed her.

"Whoa." West's mother sidestepped a near collision as she exited the break room with two steaming mugs. "Everything okay? You look ill."

"Yes. Bathroom."

"Oh." The woman frowned. "I was just bringing you tea. Do you want me to go with you?"

Tina shook her head. Tears welled and stung in her eyes. "No, thank you."

Mrs. Garrett offered a sad smile. "Let me go set these down, and I'll be right there to check on you."

"'Kay." Tina ducked into the bathroom under Mrs. Garrett's loving watch. She listened as the woman's footsteps faded in the distance. Then she quickly texted West. It was her last chance to help bring Lily home. Carl would surely take her phone the minute he saw her.

West—He came for me. He has Lily & I'm going.

She hurried from the bathroom to the rear exit. A big blue pickup waited in the gravel at the building's side, out of the parking lot cameras' range. Tina hit the record button on her video app and leaned the phone against the wall on top of a five-drawer filing cabinet in the hallway. She pointed the camera at the door's rectangular window.

This was it.

No more time to waste. West's mother would soon discover she wasn't in the bathroom. Carl would drive away with her baby.

She shoved the back door open with resolute determination and hustled into the darkness, hoping the angle on her phone was right, praying that West would find the video of the truck as they pulled away and follow it wherever it would take her. It was the only hope she had left.

Behind her, her phone began to ring.

Chapter Eighteen

The truck was in motion before Tina could fasten her seat belt, tossing dirt and spinning recklessly into the road beside the sheriff's department. Tina scooted closer to the car seat on the bench between her and Carl. Her heart ached to burst at the sight of her beautiful sleeping princess. "Be careful," she scolded. "You have an infant in this truck. You have to protect her." She would never let anyone hurt Lily again.

"She's f-fine."

Tina traced the five-point harness with her hands in the dark. It seemed to be correctly buckled, and the seat was secured to the bench.

Cones of light flashed over them as they headed through the center of town, making Lily's sweet face briefly visible in the darkness. An overwhelming sense of joy and relief flooded through Tina with each peek, enough to make her weep if she wasn't so terrified. Carl was right. Lily looked wonderful. Unharmed, clean and content. "Thank you," she whispered. "Thank you for taking good care of her." She stroked her sleeping baby's cheeks and hands, desperate to unhook the safety belt and bring her into her arms. Lily's tiny fist curled instinctively around Tina's finger. "I missed you, too," Tina cooed.

Carl took the next right on two wheels, blowing through a stop sign as if it didn't exist. "I c-can't believe you ca-came," he said with unbridled awe. "I mean, I kn-kn-knew you would, but I was still afraid I—I might be wr-wrong. You know?"

As if he'd left her a choice. Taking a picture of her baby and threatening to never let her see her again. How could she *not* have come to him?

Tina measured her breaths and watched in fear as Carl drove maniacally through the night. Then again, he didn't need to worry about getting pulled over. He'd led the entire sheriff's department to the other side of town. "Carl? Please slow down."

"I know how to dr-drive," he snapped.

"Okay." She quickly agreed. "But you're scaring me. I haven't seen either of you in a while, and I want us to be safe."

"Oh." Carl eased his foot slightly off the gas. "Sorry."

"Thank you." The Thank You for Visiting Shadow Point sign came and went, disappearing behind them in a flash. Tina tallied the turns as they left town, mentally cataloging the convoluted route as long as she could, but she was officially lost. "Where are we going?"

"Home."

She bit her tongue against the obvious. There didn't seem to be any homes where they were going.

Just darkness. Forest. And the endless curving road. Soon, a Leaving Cade County sign came and went, as well. Her stomach soured. How far had they gone? Where would they go? "I should stop and get some things," she said. "I didn't have time to pack."

He slowed at a crossroads and turned his face to hers. His expression was shrouded in shadows, much like his intent. "D-don't worry about th-th-that. I'm taking care of you now. Once you get comfortable here, you—you can take care of m-me, too. We're a family now." He reached over Lily's car seat for Tina's cheek, and she jumped.

Her opposite shoulder hit the door. She was out of room in the cab.

Carl replaced his hand on the steering wheel. Rejection colored his cheeks. He twisted his grip on the wheel until his knuckles were bone white. "This isn't h-how I wanted us to start our l-l-life together. I had plans. Better ones. Smoother ones, but—but I think you can still be happy if y-y-you give it a try." He checked his rearview mirror before turning onto an unlit section of a winding mountain road.

They rocked and bumped along a dark gravel lane beside a field of wildflowers for several minutes. Tina recognized the trail as a driveway when a small bungalow came into view, almost completely hidden among the trees.

"Surprise," he said, shifting the truck into Park beside a four-wheeler.

Tina gripped Lily's car seat instinctively. "What is this place?"

The porch light was on and an aged swing hung from the rafters. Nothing and no one else was visible between Tina and the horizon. Just fields and trees and night.

"My old b-babysitter lived here. I spent a lot of time with her when my m-m-mother was gone or had her boyfriends over. If they didn't like me, I—I came here." He opened the driver's-side door.

Tina watched as Carl rounded the truck's hood and headed for her side. He knocked hard on the window with one bent knuckle.

She released the seat belts on the car seat and herself. "Are you sure we're allowed to be here? Is it yours?" It couldn't be his, legally anyway. West would've checked for properties owned by Carl or his mother as soon as Lily went missing. He opened the door and offered his hand.

Tina climbed out with a shiver. She clutched Lily's carrier to her chest. "What happened to the sitter?"

"She died."

Tina took another look at the home. "When?"

"A few years ago. Before you and I m-met outside the coffee shop." Carl pressed a palm to the small of her back, urging her forward.

That explained a lot. With his mom sick and his preferred mother figure dead, he'd needed to fill that void fast, and Tina was everything he'd hoped for. She'd even showed him kindness when he was still a stranger. She chewed the insides of her cheeks in frustration. Kind deeds were supposed to better the world, not crumble hers.

Tina moved slowly, carefully, toward the building where anything could happen to her or her daughter and no one would ever know. Strips of white paint curled away from the wood. The porch steps were tilted and sunken from age and neglect. "Your baby-sitter left her home to you?"

"N-no. It belongs to her daughter." He added pressure to her back, forcing her to pick up the pace. "She lives out of state and h-h-hates the thought of the place standing empty like this. It needs a family to care f-for it, to make memories in it like my s-s-sitter and I did."

Tina doubted that her captivity at this place would be the magical experience the woman had in mind. She moved carefully up the crooked steps. "I really wish I had a few of my things," she said in an attempt to stall. "I've never stayed anywhere without taking at least a toothbrush. Maybe there's a little store nearby. We could run in for a few supplies. Is there someplace like that?" A place where she could signal the clerk for help, or make a run for it with Lily? Someplace well lit and public or somewhere they could disappear into the night and wait for dawn. She wasn't picky as long as she and Lily had a fighting chance at freedom.

"No need." Carl turned the doorknob and motioned her inside. "I t-told you. I've taken care of everything."

The home's interior lights flickered on, and Tina blinked to make sense of the scene before her. The sheets covering musty old furniture were topped with afghans and throw pillows like the ones from her home. Even the rug beneath the coffee table and magazines spread on top were all hers. No, not hers exactly, but all replicas, purchased by a man who'd taken great care to re-create a place she loved.

"What do you think?" he asked, flipping a series of shiny new deadbolts on the door behind him.

Tina tried not to wonder if he'd installed bars on the windows, too. "It's lovely," she croaked. Fear and distress tugged at her composure. Her thoughts shredded as she visually toured the room, pretending to appreciate his work.

Reminders of home were everywhere. The lamps and art were so similar to her own that her skin crawled at the sight of them. She'd never seen anything this twisted outside a horror film.

Carl was far more unstable than she'd dared to imagine. Even after the shooting. Even after everything. This creepy house, the time and detail he'd put into it, was evidence of a man beyond her help. Somewhere along the line, Carl had snapped. His reality had skewed. And trying to talk him out of this would only cause her and Lily harm.

Tina needed time to think. The baby carrier was heavy in her arms, and Lily was sure to wake up eventually. Escaping would be much easier with a quiet baby than a crying one. "Would it be rude if I said I was ready for bed?" She forced a smile. "It's been a rough couple of days, and I'm wiped out. I should probably rest now and start getting acclimated to my new home in the morning."

Disappointment clouded Carl's face. "We—we just

got here. Maybe a shower will help w-wake you up."
He moved to a door in the hallway beyond the kitchen
and flipped the light switch. A slow smile replaced
his dismay. "Take a look."

Tina inched closer. The outdated bath had pink
and black tile, a drippy faucet and loads of fresh hy-
giene products. Coordinating towels and accessories
on the counter matched her shower curtain and bath-
mat at home.

Tears blurred her eyes, and she disguised them
with a yawn, wiping away the drops with the pad of
her thumb.

Carl lifted a pink shower caddy. "Toothbrush,
paste, floss, s-soap, shampoo." He pointed to all her
favorite brands. "I left your f-f-feminine products
under the sink. I know you'll need them soon, and
you're modest. I d-d-didn't want to make you uncomfortable. Though, the woman at the store thought
I was pretty great for b-buying them for you. She
said more m-men should do things like that for their
wives."

Tina pressed her back against the wall and shifted
Lily's carrier in her aching arms. Had Carl's delusion gone so far that he imagined them married? "I
just need a minute," she said, shooting a meaningful
look at the toilet.

"Oh." He smiled. "Right. Of course." He gripped
Lily's carrier.

Tina held tight. "What are you doing?"

"P-putting her in her room. I'll m-make us something in the kitchen while you sh-sh-shower and clean

up. I bought you a new n-nightgown. I thought you'd want to start fr-fresh. Wearing something that other men hadn't…" He trailed off. "I l-left it on the bed."

Tina increased her hold on the infant carrier. "Maybe you should show me our rooms first."

Carl's smile returned. He relented his grip, leaving Tina to carry Lily, and moved to the next door in the hallway. He flipped the light switch inside. "Ta-da."

A buzzing overhead light illuminated Lily's nursery. The bedding and mobile, curtains and toys from Lily's room at Mary's home were all present.

Carl knelt before her and reached for Lily.

Tina stepped back, but he caught the carrier's handle in his hands and shot her a warning look. "It's p-past her bedtime," he grumped. "She needs to learn to slee-slee-sleep in her bed."

"I was hoping to sleep with her tonight," Tina said. "I've missed her so much." She fixed him with her most desperate stare. "Please don't take her from me again." A tear slipped over her cheek.

Carl removed Lily from the carrier and put her in the crib. He pointed to the door, indicating Tina should leave.

Tina inched backward. A hole punched through her heart as Carl pulled the nursery door shut behind them.

"Now, ou-our room," he said.

The next door he opened had a tall double bed inside. The room's decor was simple, almost thoughtless in comparison to the others he'd so meticulously staged. In fact, nothing about it reminded her of home.

Carl sat on the bed's edge and patted the space beside him. "I thought you c-could decorate this space. The bedroom at y-your house was designed for y-y-your other marriage. This one should be special. For us." He scooped a length of white fabric into his hand and held it out to her.

She took it up for inspection. "A nightgown." As promised. The delicate fabric was nearly sheer, with a scoop neckline and enough length to cover her thighs. There was no way she was ever going to wear it.

"T-try it on," he said.

"Now?" Absolutely not. She didn't like the implication, or the fact that she couldn't make a midnight escape through fields and trees in a sheer nightgown. She'd die of hypothermia before she found the road.

"Yes, please." Carl smiled. He scooted back on the bed and laced his fingers behind his head. "Sh-show me that you like it."

Tina set the gown at his feet on the bed and crossed her arms over her middle. "Modest. Remember." She backed toward the door. "Maybe we should talk first. Get to know one another better."

Reluctantly, Carl eased off the bed. He joined her at the door and slid his palm against hers, then clamped his fingers down. "I kn-know we're moving a little fast, but y-you like it like this. Y-you only knew Thomas a short while before g-getting married. You were b-barely married for five m-m-minutes before conceiving Lily." He dropped his gaze to leer briefly at her body before returning the heated gaze to her face. "We can m-make babies together, too.

Give Lily brothers and sisters. Raise th-them here." He lifted their joined hands and pressed a kiss against her knuckles.

Tina tried not to vomit.

He pulled her toward the kitchen and dragged a chair away from the table. "Sit." He went to the counter to set up the coffee maker.

Tina took a seat. With such attention to detail, she wished he'd included a block of knives like the one on her counter at home. At the moment, what she really wanted was to stab him before he mentioned the nightgown or baby making again. She watched the wall separating her from Lily. She hadn't even gotten to hold her. She'd just gotten her back and he'd taken her again. Slow tears rolled over Tina's cheeks, and she swiped them away.

He smiled at her from his position beside the coffee maker. "Do—do you remember when w-we met? You bought me coffee, then w-waved at me wh-when you pulled away. I didn't know w-why until the lady at the window said you b-b-bought my drink. I followed you home to thank you, but I wasn't br-br-brave enough to do it. It takes me t-t-time to warm up to new people." His cheeks flushed, and he turned back to the coffee.

He finished up, and the machine chugged to life. "I tried to talk to you for a c-couple weeks before I m-made up my mind. I was going to d-do it the day you went to the g-garden center for those redbud trees."

"The day I met Thomas," she said. A flood of nostalgia and grief washed over her. Thomas had been so kind. He was there for mulch and saw her struggling with the trees. "He dropped everything to help me." Then he'd followed her home to unload them. A frown tugged her lips. She'd made lemonade and served it on the porch because she knew better than to invite a stranger inside. Thomas was nice, but he wasn't her soul mate, and he was dead now because of her.

Carl selected two mugs from the cupboard with undue roughness, banging them on the counter until Tina was certain he'd wake Lily. "He h-helped himself to my girl is what he—he did. I couldn't f-forgive it. I had to be a man, stake claim to what w-w-was mine."

"You killed him."

"I removed him from our situation." Carl poured the small amount of brewed coffee into a mug and carried it to the table for her. "His loss h-hurt you for a while, I know, b-b-but you're better now. Ready to start again, I think. That was w-why I had to be pre-emptive with Steven. He'd only been to gr-group a few times and you were sp-sp-spending all your attention on him." He went back for a second mug and drained the pot's contents once again. "You know that old s-saying. Fool me once, shame on you. Fool me twice—" he pointed at his chest "—sh-shame on me. I couldn't watch you m-m-marry someone else again. That would have been my fault."

"I was never interested in Steven romantically," Tina argued. "You know I won't have a personal relationship with anyone in my care. It's unprofessional."

She'd told Carl that when he joined the group and asked her if she wanted to join him for a walk.

"Those men were all wr-wrong for you." He sighed dramatically. "Speaking of men who are wr-wrong for you. I don't like the w-w-way you look at the sheriff. I can tell he wants you. Wants this." Carl motioned between them and around the room. "N-not going to happen."

"Is that why you shot him?" she asked, chin quivering. "You didn't need to do that. You shouldn't hurt people."

He lifted and dropped one shoulder. "I saw—saw you with him. You t-touch him when he's near. Lean on him. You've only kn-known him for a few days, but y-you chose to lean on him instead of me." The accusation was thick and strong in his voice and stare.

"I've known Sheriff Garrett all my life," she said, hoping not to set him off. "I grew up in Shadow Point. With him."

Carl seemed to consider the idea. "I didn't know that."

"It's true." She lifted her mug, unable to drink, but unwilling to anger him further by refusing it completely.

"You grew up there, but d-don't have family there?" He cocked his head, maybe wondering if she'd lied.

"I used to." A tight knot formed in her throat, and she set the mug aside.

"Well, I f-forgive you for leaning on the sheriff," he said. "I kn-know what it's like to be l-l-lonely and m-make bad choices. If Sheriff Garrett is familiar to you, it m-makes sense that you'd confide in him, especially once he'd inserted himself into y-your life." Carl leaned across the table and cupped her hands in his. "B-b-but, Tina, neither of us w-will ever have to be alone again."

Her skin crawled and her stomach churned. "I can't be with my patients, unprofessionally. You know that. I could lose my license."

Carl squeezed her hands hard. "Y-you aren't g-going back to work. I'm going to take care of you and L-Lily, and you're g-going to take care of me." He released her hands with an apologetic smile and moved to stand behind her chair. The calloused skin of his palms scraped over the back of her neck and across her shoulders as he kneaded the bunched muscles there. "I only ask-asked to participate in your group to get c-close to you. I thought you kn-knew that when y-you interviewed me." He gathered the length of her hair in one hand and planted a hot, wet kiss at the nape of her neck. "Mmm."

Tina clamped her teeth together, bucking against the instinct to fight. Lily was in the next room. She had to think of Lily. She had to win Carl's trust and escape with her baby.

He dragged his sticky tongue up her neck until it reached her earlobe.

She dug her nails into her legs as he suckled and winced at the welcomed distraction.

"Gives you a shiver, huh?" he asked. "You l-like that?"

"We weren't finished talking," she said, wiggling

away. She needed to busy his mind before he re-membered the bed and nightgown that waited in the next room. "Tell me why you went to my place after the shooting. That was you who ran from the house, right? You set the table for two while you were in there."

He tugged sharply on her hair, still wrapped in his fist. "Y-you were supposed to come home alone. I was there to com-comfort you. To listen. I thought we c-could eat, and you could tell me about the tr-trauma. I was going to be your strong shoulder and hero, but y-you brought the sheriff."

He dropped her hair and gripped the back of her chair instead, yanking it roughly away from the table. "Let's dance." He set his phone on the counter and piped a slow country song through the speaker.

Tina needed that phone.

Carl wound one hand over the small of her back and pushed hair off her shoulder with the other. He lowered his mouth to her skin and kissed a disgust-ing path along her neck. "Y-you taste like honey."

She held her breath, begging her addled mind to create a plan.

"It can be like this for us every night," he said, kissing her jawline and chin, moving steadily toward her mouth.

Tina squirmed harder against his advances. "I still need that shower or maybe a hot bath." A bath would buy her more time to get herself and Lily out the win-dow without him noticing.

Carl's hands slid beneath the hem of her shirt and skimmed her sides. "I could help."

"No!" She lunged backward, instantly horrified by both his touch and her loud reaction. Her gaze jumped to the far wall separating the kitchen from Lily's room. "Sorry," she whispered. "I'm not ready. It's too soon." Suffocating fear silenced her words.

Carl moved slowly in her direction. "I d-didn't mean to scare you. I w-w-would never h-hurt you, Tina. N-not ever. You and Lily, you're my l-l-life now." He pulled her to him again and kissed her roughly. Holding her face between his palms.

Heavy tears rolled down her cheeks as she resigned herself to the worst possible fate. She wouldn't be able to escape with Lily tonight. For Tina, tonight would be about survival.

WEST CREPT ALONG the porch of a dilapidated bungalow in Cress County. It wasn't his jurisdiction, but he didn't care, and he had a team of FBI agents in play to back him up. Tina's text had stopped them before they reached the cabin at the lake and sent them back to the station at full speed. Her camera had caught the top of the blue pickup truck speeding away, but what had saved the day was her phone's presence. A quick search for the number that had sent her the photo of Lily was all tech ops had needed to trace the burner phone all the way to Carl's hideout.

He pressed his back to the wall and peered into the front window. His pounding heart nearly stopped when he saw Tina's tears. Carl Morgan kissed her mouth like the sociopath he was while she cried.

West moved to the slanted porch steps and gave them a kick.

"What was that?" Tina's voice was high and loud inside the home. Desperation had eradicated her cool exterior, leaving sheer panic on her face and tongue.

West moved into the shadows as Carl crept silently toward the window.

Carl glared through the glass. "Go to Lily's room and lock the door," he barked. "Make a single sound, or try anything stupid, and she'll pay for it. Understand?"

West ground his teeth. He hopped over the porch's railing and raced along the side of the house toward the back.

He peeked into each window in search of Tina, but found plywood nailed over the glass every time. Carl had imprisoned her and her baby. West looked behind him, wishing he could be the one to take Carl down, but Tina and Lily were his priorities.

The front door opened and snapped shut. Carl was coming, probably with a rifle.

West hurried silently onto the back porch.

Footfalls pounded over the floorboards on the other side of the rotting wooden barrier. The knob turned and Tina rushed into view, a crying baby clutched to her chest.

She squeaked at the sight of him, dressed head to toe in black. Recognition dawned slowly as he raised a finger to his lips and reached for her arm.

Lily squirmed and fussed. The sound gonged and echoed like a beacon in the darkness. "Hurry," West whispered. He gripped her elbow and pulled her in a sweeping arch back toward the road, giving the house a wide berth.

Tina shushed her frightened baby as they ran.

The telltale sound of a snapping branch stopped West short. He widened his stance, pushing Tina behind him.

"Nice try, Sheriff," Carl snarled. He stepped into view from the small grove of apple trees beside the home. "I heard you out front, and I followed you around back. Stupid move, leaving your cruiser in the drive." He sent an angry look Tina's way. "Didn't I tell you I wouldn't let him take what's mine?" He raised the barrel of his rifle to West's head.

"No," Tina cried, "please don't. Don't do this."

A thunderous crack interrupted her plea and ignited Lily's screams.

Tina's eyelids fell shut, and she sobbed against her baby's head.

Carl made a strangled sound before dropping his rifle. His expression went blank as he crumbled to the ground.

TINA'S EYES SHOT OPEN.

West wound an arm around Tina as Cole emerged from the darkness.

Cole kicked the rifle away from Carl's body. "I know it's not right to speak ill of the dead, but I hate this guy." He pinched the radio on his shoulder and relayed the news to their waiting teams.

West wrapped his arms around Tina and her baby. "Are you okay? Did he hurt you?"

Tears streamed over her face as she kissed Lily's cheeks a thousand times, sobbing, but not speaking.

"Come on." He led them to his cruiser in the driveway and opened the door so she could sit. "Here." He slid out of his black coat and wrapped it over her shoulders, cocooning her and Lily in his warmth.

A dozen men in black gear streamed from the trees and field, encroaching on the scene around them. SUVs and cruisers crawled over the loose gravel drive, and the low cry of an ambulance rose in the distance. The nightmare had finally ended, and the relief of seeing Tina and Lily safe was enough to knock him down.

West crouched before Tina as she cuddled Lily into contentment. Her smile lit up his world.

"I can't believe you're here," she said.

"Anything and always," he repeated the phrase that had meant so much to them in high school. The words were as true as ever for him, hopefully for her, too.

The pink bundle in her arms had closed her eyes. Her small mouth made quick little moves.

"She dreams of food," Tina said, laughing proudly through a fresh sob. "Just like her mama."

West brushed Lily's soft cheek with his fingertips, then kissed her mother's cheek. "I dream of you."

"I love you," Tina said. "It's okay if you don't feel the same."

West's heart expanded in his chest, stretching a smile across his face and warming him to the core. "I love you, too. I always have. Always will."

"I'm sorry I ran away when we were teens. I should've talked to you. You deserved the whole truth. From me."

"I don't blame you, and I don't care about any of that now."

Tina swiped a tear from her cheek. "I don't want to let my parents' failures affect me anymore. I don't want them to be an excuse I use to avoid finding happiness."

"I can make you happy," he promised.

Epilogue

Bright summer sun beamed down on the oak tree outside West's cabin. Tina adjusted the train of her borrowed gown. Once worn by West's mother and grandmother for the same occasion. The diamond wedding ring on her finger cast rainbows over the delicate material.

"Stop looking at him." Marissa, Blake's wife, laughed from behind the lens of her fancy camera. "He'll be there when we finish—this gorgeous sunlight won't."

Tina forced another smile, but her gaze drifted back to the man of her dreams, *her husband*, West Garrett. She smiled brighter, imagining she gave the sun a run for its money today. West was striking in black tuxedo pants, the sleeves of his dress shirt rolled up to his elbows. A set of identically dressed brothers laughed at his sides, passing Lily from hand to hand around their circle in a goofy version of hot potato. Mary watched with a prideful smile. She'd recovered nicely after Carl's attack, another answer to Tina's prayers.

Tucker Bixby had recovered, too, but he had a long road ahead of him. Tina's testimony had helped Tucker stay out of jail, but he was struggling to deal with the role he'd played in Lily's abduction, and that wasn't something Tina could help him with. She'd recommended a new therapist, but it wouldn't be easy for Tucker's tender heart to get past what he'd done. His silence could have cost Lily and Tina their lives.

Marissa snapped a few more shots, then looked at the little screen. "I'm a nature photographer, and I swear the forest creatures have longer attention spans than you today."

"I'm just really happy," Tina said, admitting the partial truth.

West's dad had walked her down the aisle. His mom had helped her with her hair and dress. His entire family had stepped up at their engagement, as if it was the most normal thing in the world to add another adult and a baby to the Garrett clan.

Tina was the definition of *blissful*, but Marissa was right—she was also distracted.

A loud wolf whistle drew a new smile over Tina's face.

West headed her way with their little girl in tow. Lily clapped her hands and toddled clumsily at his side on chubby fourteen-month-old legs. Her puffy white dress and matching floppy hair bow were the picture of perfection.

West kissed his sister-in-law's cheek. "Finished yet?"

"Never." Marissa scooped Lily into her arms and nuzzled her neck. "Go on," she said to the newly-weds. "I know it kills the two of you to keep your hands off one another for more than five minutes. Your whole wedding album will be kissing photos, you realize that?"

West's lips were already on Tina's. "Hello, Mrs. Garrett," he whispered against her mouth.

"Hello."

West's mom marched into view as he pulled away. "There's my beautiful grandbaby," she squeaked.

Lily struggled free of Marissa's grip, cheerfully reaching for her grandmother's arms.

"Is your daddy hogging all your attention?" West's mother asked.

"Da!" Lily agreed, head nodding. "Da! Da! Da!"

"Well, we can't have that. There's a hundred people here to see you." She turned on her pastel heels and marched back toward the crowd gathered on West's lawn. Lily clapped as they moved away.

"I think they are all here for her," West said. "She stole every heart in this place with her flower girl routine." He pressed a hand to his chest and bowed his head. "Every time she calls me Dad I think I'll die right there of happiness."

The careful rows of white chairs, once hugged in tulle, were scattered over the lawn now. Filled with folks catching up on old times and trading stories. Tina had expected sharing Lily with an entire family would be hard after having her all to herself for the first four months, but the opposite had been true. Each time Lily was doted on by another Garrett, Tina's heart grew impossibly bigger.

She scanned the smiling faces of her new family, then dared a look at her dashing husband. "I love you."

"I love you." He kissed her nose and hugged her tight. "Are you sure you didn't want a big church wedding like Blake and Marissa had?" he asked for the hundredth time.

She laughed. "This was everything I've ever wanted. My personal dream come true. Handsome husband. Supportive friends. Growing family." She pinned him with her most cheeky look.

West smiled. "Now we just need to get Cole and Ryder married off. Get Lily some cousins. Cole will be easier to work with. Let's start with him."

Tina draped her wrists over West's shoulders and tried again. "When I said the family was growing, I wasn't talking about marrying off your brothers or waiting for cousins. Though that will be nice, too."

West wrinkled his nose.

Tina's smile widened. "I meant *our* family is growing." She pulled his palm over her tummy and pressed it tight.

His jaw went slack. "I'm having a baby?" His bright blue eyes went wide with emotion. "You're— I'm gonna be a dad again?" He stared awestruck at their hands on her middle.

"Yes." Tina giggled against her husband's chest,

unable to believe her life had become so much more than she'd ever dared to dream. "I love you," she said once more, as West's protective arms banded around her.

He dropped his mouth to hers and planted a kiss to melt the sun. "Always and forever, Mrs. Garrett."

* * * * *

Look for the next book in Julie Anne Lindsey's
PROTECTORS OF CADE COUNTY
miniseries later this year.

And don't miss the previous title in the series,
FEDERAL AGENT UNDER FIRE,
available now wherever
Harlequin Intrigue books are sold!

SPECIAL EXCERPT FROM

Enjoy a sneak peek at LONE STAR BLUES,
part of the A WRANGLER'S CREEK NOVEL series
by USA TODAY bestselling author Delores Fossen.

When he learns he has a son, bad-boy rancher
Dylan Granger will do anything to prove he's
daddy material—even convince his ex that raising
the boy together might just be the best solution.
If only they can keep their focus on Corbin and
not on their still-simmering attraction...

"You're still in the Air Force?" he asked.

Dylan knew it wasn't just a simple question. There were other questions that went along with that, including the "right back in her face" reminder that deployments and overseas assignments might be good for a military officer but not necessarily for a toddler.

Jordan nodded. "I'm still in. For now. I'm being assigned to Lackland Air Force Base in San Antonio. But I've been... rethinking things."

He saw it then, the slight shift of her posture, and she glanced away. Not exactly any in-your-face gestures, but Dylan could see something simmering just beneath the surface. And he wanted to kick himself. She was rethinking things because she'd been held captive by those insurgents.

Now he was the one who had to glance away from her. Even though Jordan and he hadn't seen each other in years, she'd once been his wife. He still cared for her. Or at least he had cared before she'd done that custody-challenge throw down about a minute ago. Now he was riled, along with wishing that something that bad hadn't happened to her. But it had happened, and Dylan had to take it into account.

"Are you okay?" he asked her. And yes, he probably should have figured out a different way to ask if she'd gone bat-crap crazy because of being held captive when she was on deployment.

Jordan's eyes narrowed a little. Her mouth tightened, too, a reminder that yes, that mouth still had a way of getting his attention. That was why Dylan looked away again.

"I'm fine." Her tone was snappish, but it was like a person gushing blood saying that it was just a flesh wound. No way could she be fine after something like that, especially since it'd only happened weeks ago. Some folks didn't get over trauma like that—ever.

"I can get out of the Air Force if I want," she added a moment later, and her voice was a lot more even-keeled now. "While I'm on leave, I'm considering my options."

Well, Dylan wanted her to consider those options elsewhere. But he immediately frowned at that thought. Feeling that way wasn't right. Jordan was Corbin's family, too, and the kid would need all the support that he could get.

"If you're at Lackland Air Force Base, does that mean you won't be deployed or have to go do temporary duty somewhere?" he pressed.

Jordan shook her head. Hesitantly shook it, though. "There's still a chance something like that would happen." Her tone was hesitant, too.

That was his winning argument, all wrapped in her own words. Well, it was a winner if she stayed on active duty and took that assignment.

"So, you're saying you'll get out of the military, move back here and sue Dylan for custody," Lucian clarified. His brother didn't say it as mean-spirited and grouchy as he could have. He did it more the way he would while negotiating a business deal that he wasn't especially sold on. However, Dylan knew how Lucian wanted this particular deal to go down.

With Jordan getting custody.

*See what happens next when LONE STAR BLUES by USA TODAY bestselling author Delores Fossen goes on sale April 17, 2018.
You'll find it wherever HQN Books are sold!*

THE WORLD IS BETTER WITH

Romance

Harlequin has everything from contemporary, passionate and heartwarming to suspenseful and inspirational stories.

Whatever your mood,
we have a romance just for you!

Connect with us to find your next great read,
special offers and more.

f /HarlequinBooks

🐦 @HarlequinBooks

www.HarlequinBlog.com

www.Harlequin.com/Newsletters

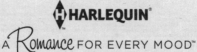

⟨H⟩ HARLEQUIN®

A *Romance* FOR EVERY MOOD™

www.Harlequin.com